"This is the gun," Clint said. "Take good care of it, okay?"

"Like it was my own," Rick replied. "How did things go over at the hotel?"

"Just fine. I got a room and nobody was the wiser. Were you able to get any information from your grapevine?"

"Our man is a very unsavory character," Rick said, frowning, "but as a gunman, second rate."

"Really?"

"No big kills to his credit. Just a long line of little ones."

"A long line?" Clint asked, hoping Cartwright hadn't gone overboard. "How long a line?"

"Well . . . rumor has it he's killed a dozen men."

Clint closed his eyes and shook his head. The job ahead wasn't going to be easy . . . .

Don't miss any of the lusty, hard-riding action in the Charter Western series, THE GUNSMITH

And coming next month:
THE GUNSMITH #65: SHOWDOWN IN RIO MALO

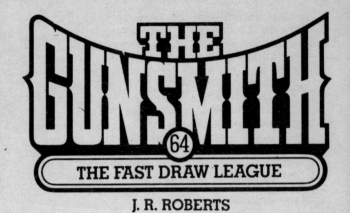

THE GUNSMITH

64

THE FAST DRAW LEAGUE

J. R. ROBERTS

CHARTER BOOKS, NEW YORK

THE GUNSMITH #64: THE FAST DRAW LEAGUE

A Charter Book/published by arrangement with
the author

PRINTING HISTORY
Charter edition / April 1987

ISBN: 0-441-30968-2

Charter Books are published by The Berkley Publishing Group,
200 Madison Avenue, New York, New York 10016.

PRINTED IN THE UNITED STATES OF AMERICA

PROLOGUE

Wes Bellman studied himself in the mirror. He had long brown hair that hung past his shoulders, sort of like the way Bill Hickok used to wear his. He had a full brown beard that covered a good portion of the lower part of his face, except for the scar on his left cheek where the hair wouldn't grow in properly. The beard was also peppered with grey.

He was tall and slender, and was wearing a buckskin-fringe jacket and dark-brown trousers. On his hip was a worn .44 Navy Colt in an equally worn leather holster.

He stepped back further from the mirror to try and take in the whole picture, then turned to the woman and man who were also in the room.

"I look ridiculous."

"That is part of the plan," Cartwright said. "If you look as if you are trying to be a cheap imitation of Hickok, someone is going to want to try you."

"I have no intentions of killing someone just to make this charade look more real."

Cartwright looked concerned.

"Well, that is unfortunate, but it's your life that you'll be putting in jeopardy. I suppose you have that right."

"Damned right I do."

1

Bellman turned and looked in the mirror again.

"I never realized that if I grew a beard it would have this much grey in it."

"We can take care of the grey," the woman said, standing up and moving up next to him. She examined him critically in the mirror.

Her name was Gloria Manners. She was a tall, dark-haired beauty who specialized in making a person look like someone else.

"What do you mean, 'take care' of it?"

"Well, we don't want anyone to wonder why a man as old as you are, and as good with a gun as you are, hasn't got a bigger reputation."

"So?"

"So, if we take the grey out of your beard you'll look younger."

You didn't seem to mind how old I was last night in bed, he thought.

She studied the hair on his head, and said, "We may have to do the same to your head. You've got a few grey hairs there, as well."

"And I've earned every one them."

"I'm sure you have, but you want to live to grow even more, don't you?

"Of course."

"Good." She turned to Cartwright and said, "We'll color his hair and beard."

"As you say."

"Jesus Christ!" Bellman said, looking in the mirror again.

Later, in bed, she said, "Look—you've even got grey hairs here."

He looked down at where she was crouched between

his legs. His penis was standing straight up, but she was studying the hair around it.

"Don't even think about it," he warned her.

"Think about what?"

"Coloring my pubic hair."

"That's all right. We can leave it alone." She patted it gently, then ran her nails along the underside of his swollen penis. "Nobody will see it, will they?"

"Well, you never know. . ."

She encircled the base of his penis with the fingers of her right hand and then lowered her mouth onto him. She sucked at him noisily, wetting the length of him thoroughly, and then took her mouth away, leaving him throbbing and bobbing in the air, red and ready for release.

"Nobody will see, will they, Wesley?"

"Well," he lied, "maybe not. . . ."

Later, when he was alone in his room, he stood in front of the mirror. The man he saw there was a stranger to him, and he began to wonder if he wasn't making a mistake.

There must have been another way to go about this. How had he let himself be talked into this charade?

He returned to the bed and settled back to replay in his mind the events that had led Wesley Bellman to this point.

ONE

Clint Adams was not disappointed to hear that Daniel Lewis Fenton had been replaced as head of the United States Secret Service. Of course, that was before he met Fenton's replacement, a snooty, officious man named William Masters Cartwright.

"Of course you understand that I loathe using personnel outside the Service," Cartwright said.

Loathe? Clint thought.

"Well, that makes us even, Mr. Cartwright, I'm 'loath' to work for the Service. I always have been. In fact, nothing I've ever done in the past has been for the Service. It's been out of friendship for Jim West."

"You're impertinent."

"Every chance I get."

Cartwright compressed his lips and regarded Clint Adams across the desk in his newly acquired office.

"I understand that you and West are friends."

"I'm glad. Then we'll have no illusions about why I'm here."

"No, of course not," Cartwright said.

The reason Clint was in Washington, of course, was that Jim West had asked him to come. Some people may have felt that West was abusing their friendship whenever he drafted the Gunsmith into the service of the

5

United States, but in truth he only did so when he felt that Clint Adams was the ideal man for the job, and Clint knew that.

"You want to give me the pitch?" he asked Cartwright.

Clint had only met Cartwright ten minutes ago. By now he felt that the man was merely a Fenton clone: well dressed, well mannered, and unsure of how to handle people except to talk down to them. Cartwright was in his early fifties, with grey hair that was combed to carefully cover a bald spot on the crown of his head. So he was vain, as well as officious *and* condescending.

Why, Clint wondered, didn't they just move Jim West up to head of the Secret Service? Well, that was actually an easy question to answer. For one thing, West would not mix well with the Washington elite. He was not a phony, as many of them were. For another thing, Jim wouldn't want the job. He preferred to stay in the field rather than stick himself behind some desk, where his skills would deteriorate. Better they should do that because of advancing age and not from lack of use—not that he was old. He wasn't much younger than Clint, maybe two or three years.

"The pitch?" Cartwright repeated.

"What's the *problem*."

Cartwright looked down at a sheaf of papers on his desk, as if he needed to refresh his memory before answering.

"Have you ever heard of the Fast Draw League?"

"Yes."

"What do you know about it?"

"Apparently, it's a club of some sort for people who like to show off with guns."

"That's the picture they want to present to the public," Cartwright said. "A group of fumblers who like to play with guns and who would be lucky not to shoot their own feet off."

"And that's not the case?"

"No, it's not. In the past four months there have been seven murders of prominent people in this country."

"How prominent?"

"Oh, you probably never heard of most of them, but rest assured they all had a place in the growth of this country. Some of them were businessmen, some politicians—"

"Senator Gorman?"

"Yes, Senator Gorman."

Senator Ed Gorman had been shot to death a month earlier while walking down a Washington street. Witnesses said that he had been accosted by a man who had shouted obscenities at him, and had then drawn a gun. The senator, who, it was rumored, always carried a gun, apparently had tried to defend himself, but the man had shot him twice and then fled.

"He is probably the best known of the people I'm talking about."

" 'People'," Clint repeated. "Then we are not just talking about men?"

"No. One woman was killed. Her name was Daisy Sheffield. She was the editor of a newspaper in Texas that had begun to do a series of articles on the Fast Draw League. It seems that Mrs. Sheffield suspected there was something about the League that wasn't all that innocent."

"I guess she was right. You said *Mrs.* Sheffield?"

"She was a widow."

"How did her husband die?"

"Naturally—about six years ago. His death does not figure into this."

"Now tell me how you figure the Fast Draw League fits in."

"We've uncovered some information that leads us to believe that they might be training professional killers, who they then hire out for pay."

"And who was it who uncovered this information?"

"Your friend, Jim West."

To Clint, that made the information as good as gold.

"Where do I fit in?"

"We want to send in someone to infiltrate the Fast Draw League, either as an instructor, or a would-be-student."

"This was Jim's idea?"

Cartwright cleared his throat and said, "Yes, it was."

"Why doesn't he do it himself? He's pretty handy with a gun."

"He is approaching the matter from another angle."

"Which is?"

"He is in Texas, looking into Mrs. Sheffield's death. He's trying to find out just what kind of information she had on the League. Oh, don't get me wrong—he wanted to go in, but I prefer to employ his investigative talents. I, uh, then asked him to recommend someone who we could send in, and he said there were only two other men he knew who could do the job."

"Me, and Talbot Roper."

"Yes," Cartwright said, wondering how Clint had known that.

"Roper would want to be paid."

"That was what Mr. West said. He decided—uh, I asked him to contact you."

"Of course."

There were other men Clint knew of who might be able to do the job—Warren Murphy, "the Irish Gun," came to mind, and Fred Hammer, if they had needed a black man—but Clint was probably the only one who would do it for nothing, out of friendship for West.

"Well, how do you feel about this, Mr. Adams?"

"I would do it, except for one thing."

"What is that?"

"If this Fast Draw League is a school for killers, as you seem to think, then somebody who knows what he's doing is teaching them. Someone like that might know who I am and recognize me on sight."

"Jim West—uh, we thought of that."

"You did?"

The man pressed a button on his desk which, Clint assumed, transmitted a signal elsewhere. A moment later the door opened and a woman stepped in.

She was tall, dark-haired, fairly young, with long legs and full breasts. In fact, her breasts appeared to be too large for her otherwise slender frame, but the effect was rather startlingly attractive.

"This is Gloria Manners. Miss Manners, Clint Adams."

"I'm happy to meet you, Mr. Adams," she said, extending her hand to shake like a man.

Clint stood and took her hand, which he found to have a firm grip.

"I've heard a lot about you."

"Some good, I hope."

"Most of it."

That must have meant that she heard it from Jim West. Pillow talk? he wondered. The woman appeared to be West's type—attractive and intelligent.

"Miss Manners specializes in—" Cartwright groped for the proper words, then said, "Oh, you explain it to him."

She smiled at Clint, who found her mouth to be exceptionally wide—almost too wide, but not quite.

"I take people's faces and make them look different."

"How do you do that?"

"Well, I use what's there—hair, mostly, changing the way it looks and such—and then I add makeup."

"Makeup?"

"Yes. I'm sure you've been to the theater and seen how actors and actresses can change their appearance by use of makeup. I use it in much the same way. I can change the shape of a person's nose, or chin, or even the shape of their face."

"That's very interesting."

"In your case, for instance," she went on, studying his face now, "I'd recommend letting your hair grow longer, and also growing a beard. That would do wonders for your appearance."

"Improve it, you mean?"

She grinned impishly and said, "I didn't say that, but it would certainly change it."

Clint turned and looked at Cartwright.

"We can give you a new name, and circulate a somewhat small, yet effectively unsavory, reputation; something that would appeal to the League. What do you say?"

He studied Cartwright for a moment, then decided it was much more pleasant to look at Gloria Manners.

"Well, I suppose it would necessitate my putting myself in this young lady's capable hands?"

"It would," Cartwright said, although his tone clearly indicated that he thought that was the wrong reason to do it.

It was as much to piss Cartwright off as for anything else, that Clint said, "In that case, I'll do it."

TWO

Four days later, the desk clerk in Clint's hotel began to look at him funny.

Women began to give him funny looks in restaurants.

Clint walked out of his hotel after a week with beard stubble on his face, and the hair on his neck curling up at the base of his collar. He knew that if he were walking down the streets of Dodge City or Abilene, no one would give him a second look. Here in Washington, however, a disheveled man walking the street, and staying in one of Washington's finest hotels, was not a common sight.

He made his way to a building on Q Street, which housed the United States Secret Service. Actually, they only had a few offices in the building, one of which was used by William Masters Cartwright. In the lobby of the building, he met with Gloria Manners.

"You look fine," she said, inspecting him.

They had agreed that they would meet there in a week to see how his beard and hair were progressing.

"I look like a mess."

"That's what I mean." She walked around him and said, "Luckily, you needed a haircut when you got here, so your hair is coming along fine. And your beard grows in pretty quickly, doesn't it?"

13

"Is that all I came here for? To be inspected like an animal for sale?"

"No, I'd like you to come upstairs with me. I have a room."

"Oh, really?"

She frowned at him, then understood and smiled an embarrassed smile.

"I didn't mean to imply—I mean I have a room where I work."

"I see."

"I want to see what we can do with makeup."

"You know, I'd really rather not have anything to do with makeup—"

"It's not this kind of makeup," she said, touching her own face. "Come upstairs and let me show you what I mean."

"All right."

He followed her up a flight of stairs and into a room that had several mirrors on the walls, and a small table in front of each mirror. On either side of the mirrors were small gas lamps.

"Sit in front of one of the mirrors."

"Look, Miss Manners—"

"If I'm going to be altering the shape of your face, the least you can do is call me Gloria."

"All right, Gloria. This makeup thing—"

"It's greasepaint."

"What?"

"That's what they call it in the theater. It's makeup with a grease base. All it does in the theater is highlight what's already there. I use it to *change* what's there."

"Like what?"

"Let me show you. Sit down."

He frowned, but removed his hat and jacket and sat down.

She began to surprise him.

She applied some greasepaint and suddenly his face was hollowed out underneath his cheekbones, changing the way he looked.

"That's amazing."

"Watch this," she said.

She took some putty and applied it to the sides of his nose, and suddenly he had a much flatter, wider nose, giving his face an entirely different appearance.

"This is like magic," he said. He leaned forward and touched his nose, smearing the putty. "Except for that."

"Well, that's a problem, all right. You'd have to make sure nobody smeared you or hit you—"

"Well," he said, standing up. "I guess we're just going to have to make do with the long hair and beard."

"What do you mean?"

"Where I'm going, Gloria, I'm liable to have a lot of close contact, even physical contact. I can't be having grease or putty on my face that's going to give me away at a crucial moment. I wouldn't live ten minutes."

"That may be," she said, "but if they find out who you really are—"

"I'm going to be there all alone, with nobody to fix my makeup. No, Miss Manners. I'm afraid that when it comes to my life, I'll call all the shots."

"You're tying my hands."

"There must be other ways you can use."

"Well," she said, "I could teach you to walk. . . ."

"You could what?" he asked, not sure that he had heard here correctly.

"I could show you a different way to walk, how to hold yourself differently, make yourself look like a different man—at least, from behind. I can also show you how to alter your speech pattern."

"When can we start that?" he asked.

"Today, if you like."

"How about tonight at dinner?"

"Dinner," she said, shaking her head. "I don't usually associate with the men in the Service—"

"I'm not in the Service, Gloria," he pointed out. "Besides, I haven't been able to get a woman to eat with me. Not the way I look."

"I don't wonder," she said, smiling. "All right, Mr. Adams, I'll have dinner with you."

"That's something else we're going to have to change."

"What's that?" she asked.

"I'm going to need a new name. You can't do that with makeup."

"We'll think of one."

THREE

Gloria Manners chose the restaurant, an out of the way place on a darkened side street.

After they had been shown to their table, Clint leaned over it and said, "I get the feeling you're ashamed of me."

"Of course not—" she started to reply, then realized that Clint was kidding. "You mean the fact that this place is so out of the way?"

"Yes."

"It's used by some of the men in the Service."

"You say the word 'Service' as if you were saying 'Heaven.' "

"Do I? I never noticed."

"How do you feel about it?"

"The Service?"

"See, you did it again. Yes, I mean the Service."

Her eyes lit up, but a waiter came over before she could speak.

"You've been here before," Clint said. "Order for both of us."

She ordered very simply—steaks, potatoes, biscuits and coffee—and then, as the waiter left, that look came into her eyes again.

"I want to work in the field."

"Really?"

She nodded.

"Mr. Fenton said I would, eventually."

"Fenton. But he's gone, now. What does Mr. Cartwright say?"

Suddenly, she looked worried.

"I haven't discussed it with him—but surely, if Mr. Fenton said—"

"I have a feeling that Mr. Cartwright has a mind of his own, Gloria. If I were you, I'd talk to him about it."

"Maybe I will."

"But then again, if I were you I wouldn't be so anxious to go out into the field. It's pretty dangerous out there."

"But that's what makes it so exciting, isn't it? If there were no danger—"

"If there were no danger this would be a nicer world to live in, Gloria. You should live your life without ever having to be in danger."

"But how can you say something like that? You, with the reputation you have?"

"Reputations are cheap. Look at what Cartwright said. He's going to create a new one for me, just like that. With a few well-placed words."

"But they say that you're the 'Gunsmith,' the fastest gun alive."

"How can anyone know that, unless I've faced every man who is now living?"

"But that would be impossible to do."

"Then how could I lay claim to such a reputation?"

She stared at him as if he had just desecrated a holy shrine.

"Think about it."

She did, over dinner. The steaks were tough, the

potatoes hard and the biscuits even harder. The coffee, however, was good, and that almost saved the meal for him.

"Well?" he asked.

"It was terrible, I know," she said, "but I never said the food was good. I just said that a lot of the men from the Service use it."

"No, I mean what do you think about what I said?"

She shrugged.

"I guess you're right. . .but I would still like to try working in the field."

"Well, if you're patient enough, you might get your chance. Now tell me, how do we change the way I walk and talk. . . ?"

After they left the restaurant, he practiced walking and talking with her on the dark streets of Washington.

"Keep your lips together when you speak, and clip your words—"

"You. . .mean. . .like. . .this. . . ?"

"Just like that."

"I can't do that."

"Why not?"

"It hurts."

"Clint. . .try it again."

Later, they tried the walk.

"No, no—more weight on the front of your feet. You walk with your weight back, so if you're going to be somebody else, you have to walk with your weight forward."

He tried it.

"That's better, but bend your back so you look shorter. No, no—round out your shoulders more. . . . that's it. . .you're getting better."

"Here we are," he said, abruptly.

"Where?"

"My hotel."

She gave him a slow look, then looked up at the four-story concrete building. Over the doorway, etched into the concrete, it said D. C. HOUSE.

"Your hotel."

"Yes, I have a room here."

"An expensive room, too, I'll bet."

"Well, after all, your Service is picking up the tab for it."

"Yes."

"It's really a very nice room."

She regarded him silently for a few moments, and then said, "And?"

"I'd like you to come upstairs with me."

"And, of course, you certainly don't mean to imply anything—"

"Oh, but I do. I mean to imply quite a bit," he said, correcting her. "This beard stubble and the unruly hair have played hell with my sex life, Gloria."

"Is that a fact?"

"It certainly is. Why, you don't know how deprived I've been."

"I can just imagine. . ."

"The tension I feel has been almost unbearable. You can't send me into the field with all this sexual tension built up inside of me. What would happen if I got killed because of it? You'd never be able to forgive your—"

"Okay."

"Okay?"

"Okay. You've convinced me. I'll go upstairs with you."

"But I haven't finished my spiel yet," he said. "I mean, I haven't even gotten to the part where I break into tears and mention my mother—"

"We'd better hurry up before I change my mind."

"I have to warn you," he said. "The desk clerks here have been giving me disapproving looks ever since I stopped shaving."

"Well, that's certainly not going to change when we walk in together, is it?"

They went into the lobby of the hotel and walked to the stairway under the stern gaze of a middle-aged desk clerk.

Upstairs, Clint led the way to his room and then stopped in front of the door.

"Last chance to back out."

"I can't back out."

"Why not?"

"It's my job."

"Your job?"

She nodded.

"I'm changing the way you look, the way you walk— why, Clint, it's my job to make sure I change the way you do. . .everything."

FOUR

"Your beard rubbed my thighs raw."

"It did not. Look," he said, running his tongue over her inner right thigh, and then the left. "See, not raw at all. Really very sweet, in fact."

"Yes."

"But not as sweet as. . .this. . ."

His tongue probed her, and since it was only moments after her orgasm, she was very sensitive.

"Sweet," he said, licking her moist slit until his tongue touched her clit.

"Yes. . ." she said. And then, ". . .oh yes. . ."

He began to lap at her then, as if he were the kitty and she the milk, and she lifted her butt off the bed to meet the pressure of his tongue.

"Ooh. . ." she moaned.

"Sensitive?"

"Yes."

"Want me to stop?"

"Never!"

So he didn't.

He got his nose wet, and his cheeks, and then she was bucking underneath him. He used his elbows to pin her thighs down, and the inability to move seemed to heighten the sensations she was feeling.

"Oh, God, you've got to. . .let me. . .move. . ."

"No, I don't," he said, his voice muffled. "I don't, at all."

"No," she agreed then, "you don't. . . . Ooh. . . ."

"What I want to know," he said a few moments later, "is why you say, 'ow, ow, ouch' at the most crucial moment."

"Don't make fun!" she scolded him, slapping him on the chest.

"I'm not making fun," he said. "I really want to know."

"Well, because it hurts."

"Then you should be telling me to stop."

"No."

"Why not?"

"Because it hurts so good."

She rolled on top of him and kissed him, her mouth lingering on his for a long, long time, her tongue probing, touching, seeking. . . .

"Mmm," he said. "That was good."

"If I bit you it would hurt, right?"

"Of course."

"Would you want me to kiss you again?"

"Of course."

"Even if I bit you?"

"Yes."

"Why?"

"Because a little pain is worth a lot of pleasure."

"Ah, I'm glad you feel that way," she said, sliding down his body.

"Why?"

"Because I'm going to see if you *really* feel that way. . ."

She used her mouth to cause him some of the most ex-
quisite pain he'd ever had the pleasure of enduring, only
to turn it into the most intense pleasure. . .and back to
pain. . .and then the incredible pleasure of release. . .

". . .and now I suppose you never want to see me
again," Gloria Manners said.

"Definitely not."

"After I hurt you like that."

"It was terrible."

"For me, too. I just feel so bad about doing it that I'd
like to make it up to you."

"How?"

"Oh," she said, reaching for him, "we'll find a
way. . ."

She was warm and wet and she *held* him, pulled on
him, fought him as he tried to slide out so that he could
slide into her again. Once he was in she didn't want him
to go, and she finally wrapped her long legs around him
and tightened her powerful thighs, holding him. From
there on she used her muscles to massage him, scraped
his back with her nails, bit his shoulder as he cupped her
buttocks and exploded, filling her up.

"Well," he said, stretching languidly, "now that
you've taught me how to walk differently. . .and talk
differently. . .and make love differently. . ."

"Better?"

He thought a moment, then said, "Well, different,
anyway. Now that we've done all of that, we've got to
come up with a name."

She rolled over so that she was pressed tightly against
him, and slid one arm underneath him.

"Oh, that's easy."

"It is?"

"Of course."

"Well then, don't keep me in suspense, young lady. Please, what's my name?"

"Bellman."

"Bellman? Why Bellman?"

"Well," she said, snaking her hand down between his legs, "you certainly rang *my* bell. . ."

"Bellman?" Cartwright asked.

"That's right," Clint said.

"Why Bellman?"

"Why not?"

"It doesn't have a dangerous ring to it." The man was clearly disappointed.

Give me a break, Clint thought.

"What would you suggest?"

"I don't know. Steele? Stone? Something solid, something strong."

"I like Bellman."

"Well, what's the first name, then?"

That one had been fairly easy, too. When Clint had walked Gloria Manners home the previous evening, they had walked west from his hotel to her building.

West had thus become "Wes," and two-bit gunman "Wes Bellman" was born.

"Wes Bellman."

"Wes? Why Wes?"

"It's good enough for Wes Hardin."

"I suppose."

Cartwright's disappointed frown deepened.

"I was hoping for a more powerful name, but of course the choice should be yours."

"That's the name, Mr. Cartwright," Clint said. "Start circulating my new reputation, but make sure you don't go overboard."

"Of course not. It will be just enough to get them interested in you."

"Fine."

He turned and left the office. Gloria was waiting in the lobby for him.

"What did he think of the name?"

"He was hoping for something stronger," Clint said. "Maybe we should have used 'Rock Stone'."

"Well," she said, groping for his crotch, "you were rock hard last night."

"Behave yourself, woman." He slapped her hand away playfully. "Do you want someone to see you groping a very scruffy man in public?"

"Well then, let's go someplace where I can grope you in private."

"How about your room upstairs?"

"Fine," she said, "I can get some business in at the same time."

"What kind of business?"

"Well, we have to check out Mr. Wes Bellman, don't we? Let's see if the new can stand up to the old, huh?"

FIVE

Which brought Wes Bellman to this point in time—
two days before he would head into the Southwest
armed with his new reputation, and hoping that something called the Fast Draw League would try to recruit
him.

He knew that Gloria Manners—who had been spend-
ing a lot of time with him these past two weeks in Washington—wanted to do something about the grey hair in
his beard, but he hoped to avoid that. So far he'd
avoided any effort on her part to use makeup. He
thought that with the long hair and the beard, his new
way of walking, standing, and talking, Wes Bellman
was so unlike Clint Adams that there was hardly a trace
of Adams left.

Only two things made him even slightly uncomfort-
able. First was his decision to carry his own converted
double-action Colt. He had decided to adopt a new gun
to go along with his new identity, and he'd chosen a .44
Navy Colt that he had found in a Washington gun shop.
The gun was old, but it had been well cared for, and he
worked on it even further until he was fully satisfied
with its performance.

The second decision was even more obvious than the
gun, and that was that he'd have to buy a horse and

leave his big black gelding, Duke, behind. He only hoped that he would be able to find a fairly good animal to use in Duke's place.

In general, he was satisfied with his preparations for this "favor" that he was doing for Jim West. And most of it was due to Gloria Manners. This had been their last night together, though. They had mutually agreed to that. He wanted to prepare himself emotionally for his charade, and she understood that.

He only hoped that he didn't unexpectedly run into his friend Jim West along the way.

His friend might not recognize him, and shoot him by accident.

He sat in William Masters Cartwright's office the following day, going over the final preparations.

"Your reputation has been sprinkled throughout the Southwest region, Ad—ah, Bellman. By the time you get there, you should be reasonably well-known."

"Fine. What have you heard from Jim West?"

"Only that he believes the so-called Fast Draw League is operating somewhere in Texas or New Mexico. Therefore, that's where you'll concentrate your efforts."

"Right," Clint said, because he trusted Jim West implicitly. If West thought that was where the League was operating, he was willing to start there.

"I must say that the change in your appearance is rather startling."

"Gloria Manners had a lot to do with that. You've got a good operative there, Mr. Cartwright."

"Indeed. Well, is there anything else you need before you get started?"

"No, we've gone over everything. I've got my

weapon, and I'll get my own horse once I reach Texas."

"The only intangible, then, is how you will notify us when you find the League's hideout."

"I'll have to improvise that."

"I really don't like leaving that aspect of it un-planned—"

"*You* don't like it? I'm the one going in there un-chaperoned."

"Well, we can't very well plant someone there when we don't know where the League is."

"When I find the League—if it exists—I'll get the word out. Don't you worry."

"Well, then—all that remains is to wish you good luck, and God speed."

"I appreciate the sentiment, Mr. Cartwright."

Cartwright made no effort to stand up or to shake hands, which further illustrated the point that the man did not know how to treat people. Clint wondered why only social incompetents became Director of the Secret Service.

"I'll be in touch," Clint said, rising and heading for the door.

"Good luck. . .Bellman."

That night in his hotel room, Wes Bellman once again went to work on his Navy Colt, making sure that, when it was time, it would perform properly. His modified Colt had been packed away carefully—not without some pang of remorse—and he had yet to decide what he was going to do with it while he was gone.

Duke, on the other hand, was already being taken care of in Labyrinth, Texas, by his friend Rick Hart-man, so it probably would have made sense to drop the gun off there as well. If he trusted Rick with his horse—

and he did—he would certainly trust him with his gun.

A smile spread over his face as he thought about his friend, and he wondered if Rick would be able to see through Wes Bellman to the man he really was.

It would be interesting—and fun—to find out.

He was getting ready to turn in when there was a knock on his door.

It was Gloria Manners.

"I thought we agreed to say goodbye last night," he said as she walked past him into the room.

"I did agree," she said, unbuttoning her shirt, "but I lied." He watched while she finished undressing and then, totally naked, standing with her breasts thrust forward and her hip shot to the left, she said, "Do you want to throw me out?"

He gathered her up into his arms and said, "Silly question."

SIX

It was just a little after noon when Wes Bellman rode into Labyrinth on a spotted grey gelding. He directed the horse down the main street and reined him in front of the saloon called Rick's Place. He dismounted and looked up and down the street before entering the saloon.

Inside, he walked to the bar and planted both elbows on it. The bartender looked at him and obviously disapproved of the long hair and scruffy beard.

"What can I get you?"

"I'll have a beer," Bellman said. His speech was clipped, almost as if he had something in his mouth. "And make it a cold one."

"Cold is all we've got, mister."

"Yeah."

The bartender placed the beer in front of the man, who sipped it and then brought the mug crashing down on the bar, spilling most of the contents.

"What the hell—" the bartender said. He was a big man with huge hands, and he clenched them now into fists.

"You call that cold?"

"That's as cold as it gets, friend," the bartender said,

leaning on the bar. "You don't like it, take your business somewhere else."

"I want to see the owner."

"You won't get any more satisfaction out of him than you will out of me."

"Listen, bartender," the bearded man said. He put his face about two inches from the bartender's. "I want to see the owner of this place, or there's going to be a lot of broken glass around. You got that?"

The bartender studied the man. The stranger was tall and able looking, but he was fairly sure that he would be able to take care of him—but he wasn't sure he could do it with a minimum of damage.

"All right," he finally agreed. "You want the boss, you got him—but you ain't gonna like him. Wait here."

The bartender walked to the back of the room and knocked on a door. He opened it just far enough to stick his head in, then backed out and waited. A few moments later the door opened again and Rick Hartman stepped out.

"Where is he, T.C.?" he asked.

"At the bar."

The saloon owner looked at the bar and saw the tall, long-haired man wearing a buckskin-fringe jacket. His beard looked as if it hadn't been trimmed in a while.

"I'll take care of it," he told the bartender. "Get back behind the bar and get the man another beer."

"But boss—"

"Get it."

The bartender went back behind the bar and Rick Hartman walked over to the dissatisfied man.

"You wanted to see me?"

"You the owner?"

"That's right."

"Your beer stinks."

"Is that a fact?"

The bartender put another one on the bar and Rick Hartman looked at it.

"Looks fine to me."

"It's warm."

Rick put his hand around the glass.

"It feels cold to me."

"Drink it."

Rick put the mug to his lips and sipped the beer. It was freezing.

"It's cold."

"The hell it is," the bearded man said. He picked up the glass and sipped the beer himself. "Well, I'll be damned. You're right. It is cold." He looked at the bartender and said, "That other one you gave me was warm."

The bartender looked at his boss and gave him a helpless shrug.

"Well, as long as you're satisfied now," Rick said to the man.

"Well, not quite."

"What else can I do for you?"

The bearded man leaned over, as if he were about to impart a big secret.

"You got any women around here?"

"There are plenty of women in town."

"No, I mean here, to hire."

"Maybe later in the day, friend," Rick said. "It's a little early now."

"It's never too early for a woman, friend," the bearded man said, prodding Rick's elbow with his hand. "You must have some private stock around that I could dip into."

"I'm sorry, no."

"Hey, come on—don't you know that the customer is always right?"

"Not here. Listen, friend, if I was you I'd move on. This happens to be the favorite saloon of Clint Adams, the Gunsmith."

"The Gunsmith?" the bearded man said, raising his eyebrows. "He drinks here?"

"All the time."

"Well, where is he?" the man said, looking around. "Point the legend out to me. I ain't killed me a living legend all week."

"Certainly," Rick said. "I'll be glad to point him out to you."

The bearded man looked at Rick Hartman, who poked him in the nose with his forefinger.

"He's standing right here," he said, "looking for all the world like a scruffy sheepdog."

SEVEN

"You know," Clint said later in Hartman's office, "you haven't exactly filled me with a lot of confidence about my new identity."

"Clint," Rick said, "you truly do look like shit. But believe me, I'm probably one of the only people in the world who could have recognized you."

"How did you do it?"

"We've been friends a long time," was all that Rick would say. "But look on the bright side. T.C. didn't recognize you at all. You had him fooled, at least."

"Yeah, I guess," Clint said. "Tell me—how long did it take you to spot me?"

"Right off, friend. Right off."

"Sure."

Clint dropped his hat on Rick's desk, sat in a chair and put his feet up. The hat was sweaty and the boots were covered with dust.

"Jesus, do you have to do that?" Rick picked up the hat gingerly with two fingers and dropped it on the floor.

"What is this all about, anyway?"

"I'm doing a job," Clint said, "and I don't want anyone to recognize me."

"What kind of job?"

"Have you ever heard of something called the Fast Draw League?"

"Of course. Supposedly they're a bunch of would-be gunmen who get together to practice their fast draw and target shooting."

"But?"

"But in truth, they're a top-notch training ground for gunmen and killers."

Clint looked at his friend admiringly and said, "You never cease to amaze me, Rick. How do you know all these things?"

"I keep well informed."

"That's for sure. What else can you tell me that might help?"

"Just that if you find them—and no, I can't tell you where they are—you're liable to get a couple of unpleasant surprises."

"Like what?"

"Not *what*," Rick said. "Who—or a couple of whos."

"Okay, I'll bite. Who?"

"I don't know who—I'm just saying maybe."

"Maybe what? Are we playing a game, here?"

Rick leaned forward, wrinkled his nose at his friend and leaned back again.

"All I'm saying is this: Over the past few years, one or two reputations have turned up missing. Nobody seems to know where they've gone, but the word I get is that maybe they're working for the Fast Draw League."

"As what? Killers?"

"Instructors."

"And what we're talking about here is men who might know who I am."

"People in your. . .fraternity. . .can usually identify

each other, even if you're not friends. Isn't that true?"

"My fraternity?"

"You know what I mean, Clint. You can identify a gunman even if you haven't seen him before, can't you?"

"Sometimes."

"Well, if you run into a couple of guys who know you only by rep, and from a distance, your disguise will probably hold up. If you run into an old enemy, who knows you pretty well, you may be in trouble."

Clint stared at Rick and then said, "You're just a regular little confidence builder, aren't you? You got any names?"

"Pick one. You know as well as I do who has turned up missing over the past few years. When's the last time you heard from Warren Murphy?"

"He's not missing—and he wouldn't hire out as an instructor to a bunch like that."

"What about Ron Diamond?"

"I saw him not too long ago," Clint said, "and the same goes for him."

"Well then, you pick a name."

"I'd rather not," Clint said, standing up and retrieving his hat from the floor. "If I do, I might start worrying about them."

He started for the door and said, "I'll check in with you later."

"Where are you going to be?" Rick asked. "In your room at the hotel?"

There was a room that was regularly held for Clint Adams at the Labyrinth Hotel.

"No, I'm going to keep playing this role, even here. It'll get me comfortable with it. You're the only one who will know who I am."

"Me and T.C."

"Right."

"Okay. When are you leaving?"

"In the morning."

"With Duke?"

"I can't risk that. I could be identified by someone who recognizes Duke."

"What are you going to do for a horse?"

"I've got another horse outside."

"Another gelding?"

"Sure. I don't need some horse who's going to go sniffing after every female he sees," Clint said. "I can do that myself."

"Is the horse any good?"

"He's no Duke, but I think he'll take me where I want to go."

He started for the door.

"Wait a minute," Rick said. "What's that?"

"What?"

"That," Rick said, pointing to Clint's hip.

"That's my gun. . .or, at least, the gun I'll be wearing for a while."

"What about your Colt?"

"Can't wear it for the same reason I can't ride Duke."

"What are you going to do with it?"

"Well, I was planning on leaving it with you," Clint said, and then added, "that is, if you promise not to play with it."

"Oh, I promise."

"Good. I'll come back for dinner later and leave it with you."

"Okay."

"And in the meantime you can do me a favor."

"What?"

"Check me out."

"What?"

"I mean, check around and see what you can find out about the new me."

"And just who is the new you?"

"Bellman, Wes Bellman."

"Well, Mr. Bellman, before you come back do us all a favor, will you?"

"What?"

"Take a bath."

EIGHT

When Wes Bellman returned to the saloon he was bathed, but he still wore the buckskin-fringe jacket and somewhat soiled and beaten up hat. Under his arm he had something wrapped in leather.

"Jesus," Rick said as Clint walked in, "you look like a poor man's Buckskin Frank Leslie."

"Thank you. Since Frank is a friend, I'll take that as a compliment."

"T.C., give the man a drink."

"A beer?" the bartender asked.

"Yeah, a cold one," Clint said in his Wes Bellman voice.

"Yeah, sure," the bartender said, good-naturedly.

He returned with the beer and said, "You know, you really had me going, Clint."

"Sorry about that, T.C., but do me a favor. Just call me Wes while I'm here, okay?"

"Sure, Cl—I mean, Wes."

Clint turned to Rick and said, "Here," putting the leather-wrapped package into his friend's hands.

"Is this it?"

"That's it."

"This is *the* gun?" Rick asked.

"And *the* holster," Clint said, mimicking his friend.

"Don't go overboard, Rick—just take good care of it, all right?"

"Like it was my own. How did things go over at the hotel?"

"Just fine. I got a room and nobody was the wiser. Were you able to get any information on Wes Bellman from your grapevine?"

"A very unsavory character," Rick said, frowning, "but as a gunman, second rate."

"Really?"

"No big kills to his credit, just a long line of little ones."

"A long line?" Clint asked, hoping Cartwright hadn't gone overboard. "How long a line?"

"Well, rumor has it he's killed a dozen men."

Clint closed his eyes and shook his head.

"Jesus—"

"Who did you get to seed this reputation for you?"

"Don't ask."

"Well, I think you'll be okay. . .Wes. You'll just have to do without the company of a lady for a while."

"Oh? Why do you say that?"

"Oh, come on, Wes. You may be clean now—relatively—but with your present appearance I don't think the ladies will be waiting in line for you."

"Is that a fact? You don't think that Wes Bellman could do all right with the ladies, eh?"

"Well, to be blunt. . .no!"

Clint looked around the saloon, which at this time of the evening was fairly busy.

"What are you looking for?"

"A new girl," Clint said. "Any time I'm away for more than a few weeks, you usually have a new girl."

"Well. . .I do have a new girl," Rick said, and he

began looking around himself. "There she is."

Clint looked at where Rick indicated and saw her. She wasn't really a girl, appearing to be in her late twenties, but she was an attractive redhead with an impressive pair of breasts that were interestingly displayed in a low-cut gown.

"She looks a little older than most of the girls you hire here."

"Well, it's a busy time and I was short-handed. She fills the bill, though; she doesn't know you."

"Well, the other girls wouldn't know me either, not as Wes Bellman."

"Well, I know you've been to bed with Angela, and she'd certainly recognize you once you got her there." Rick frowned and asked, "You haven't altered anything else, have you?"

"No."

"Well, if you're looking to prove a point," Rick said, "there's the lady to prove it with."

"What's her name?"

"Betsy."

"Okay."

At that moment, Betsy was simply making the rounds of the tables, taking drink orders. When she walked her breasts jiggled, so she was also busy dodging eager hands.

Clint took his beer and walked over to her. He was right behind her when she turned suddenly and bumped into him with her breasts.

"Ooh," she said, reaching up to scratch his beard, "I love a man with a beard. . . ."

Betsy's breasts were truly impressive.

She sat astride him, his erection buried to the hilt in

her, but the thing that really seemed to set her off was his beard. She had not been kidding when she said she loved a man with a beard. It had taken him only five minutes to get her to agree to meet him after work.

"I don't believe it," Rick had said when Clint had returned to the bar.

"Five minutes," Clint had said. "It was rough, but I just kept at it."

"Are you going to meet her?"

"Of course. It would be a shame to disappoint a woman like that."

Well, she hadn't been disappointed. As soon as they were in his room she had tossed off her clothes and grabbed ahold of his face. She rubbed his beard over her nipples until they were distended, and then she pushed his face down between her legs, where his beard mingled with hers while his tongue went busily to work.

Now she was sitting on him and she leaned over so he could rub his beard across her nipples again.

"Let me know when they get too sensitive, honey," he told her.

Clint Adams never called women "honey," but then again he wasn't Clint Adams—he was Wes Bellman, and Bellman did all the things that Clint Adams didn't.

"They'll never get too sensitive, baby, you just keep a-rubbin' 'em and I'll just keep a-ridin' you."

True to her word, she rode him until he couldn't contain himself any more, and when he went off inside of her she jammed herself flat on him, smothering him with her breasts and milking him for more with her insides.

"I tell you," she said moments later, "don't nobody

know how to satisfy a woman like a man with a beard.''

"What would happen if I shaved my beard?''

"You wouldn't get this little lady into bed again, cowboy.''

"Don't you think that's kind of strange?''

"I read someplace about a man who got his strength from his long hair.''

"Samson.''

"That's the fella. Well, I guess I just feel the same away about men with beards.''

She kissed him, thrusting her tongue inside of his mouth, and then rubbed her nose on his beard.

"You wouldn't disappoint little Betsy and shave, would you, Wes?''

"Honey, I wouldn't do anything to disappoint little Betsy, that's for sure.''

"Good,'' she said, pushing her nipples into his face, "then rub 'em up for me real good, baby. Betsy's ready for more.''

In the morning, Wes Bellman saddled up early and rode out. He had said goodbye to Rick Hartman the previous night, and had left Betsy sleeping in his hotel room, snoring lightly, having done her best to wear him out all night. In spite of that he had been able to get a few hours of sleep, and felt fairly refreshed for the journey to find the Fast Draw League . . . however long that journey turned out to be.

NINE

Johnny Skinner was the Fast Draw League's resident fast gun. It was his job to take the men who were brought to him and try and teach them how to get their guns out of their holsters as quickly as possible, and then fire as accurately as possible. Skinner was a man in his thirties, slender and tall, who wore black shirts because he thought they made him look more dangerous.

At the moment, Skinner was upset.

"I've had it," he said to Sam Gentry.

Gentry was another of the Fast Draw League's instructors, but he did not have the reputation that Johnny Skinner did. He was in his late twenties and had no illusions about his abilities with a gun. He was a husky man and knew that his hands were too large and his fingers too thick to ever allow him to become truly skillful with a gun. He counted himself lucky to have been accepted by the League. Which was why he didn't like to hear Skinner constantly complaining.

"What's the problem now, Skinner?"

"This last bunch of men we got—they're awful. I don't think any of them could hit the side of a barn. . . from the inside!"

Tired of listening to Skinner bitch every time he got

49

some new men to work with, Gentry said, "Well, why don't you go and tell Sharp about it."

Jason Sharp was the head man in the Fast Draw League, the one who made the rules and judged who would be accepted and who would not.

He was also the fastest gun in the League—at least, everyone but Skinner thought so.

"You think I won't go and tell him?" Skinner asked.

"I think you're all mouth, Skinner, and I'm getting tired of listening to it."

"You want to back up your mouth with your gun, Gentry?"

"Sure, pick on me," Gentry said. "Sharp is the man you should be complaining to. That's all I'm saying."

"Well, I'll tell him," Skinner said belligerently, "and I'll tell him right now."

"Go ahead."

"I'm going."

They were in the Lost Saloon in a town called Lost City, New Mexico, which the Fast Draw League used as a base of operations. Skinner pushed away from the bar and stalked out of the saloon.

This time he was going to tell Sharp off.

Jason Sharp liked women.

A handsome man, tall, with dark, curly hair, he also knew that women liked him.

The woman who was with him now was new to Lost City. In effect, she was trying to win Sharp's approval—and she was going about it the right way.

He was naked, standing in the center of his bedroom, and she was on her knees in front of him. She was a young woman in her early twenties, with long brown hair and small, brown-nippled breasts. Her mouth, however, was what was going to do it for her.

She cupped Sharp's heavy testicles in her hands and licked the spongy head of his huge erection. Running her tongue along the underside of his reddened, swollen penis, she removed one hand from his balls and wrapped it around the base of his hard shaft. Holding it steady that way, she opened her mouth and lowered it onto him, engulfing him.

She took as much of him into her mouth as she could and began to suckle him, fondling his balls as she did.

"Oh yes, Kathy," he said, putting his hands on her head and guiding her up and down on his shaft. "That's a good girl. . . ."

She began to suck on him noisily, guessing correctly that the sound would excite Sharp even more. He loved to hear women working on him. He believed that the louder they were, the more they were enjoying themselves.

He steadied his legs now as he felt the rush beginning, and her head began to bob faster and faster. He moved his hips in unison with her and then he was shooting forcefully into her mouth. She sucked and swallowed everything he had to give her, and then continued to suck and lick him, as if she wanted more.

"All right, all right," he said, easing her head away from him.

"Was it all right, Mr. Sharp?" she asked, looking up at him eagerly.

"It was fine, Kathy. It was just fine. Come on, get up now."

She stood up, tall and slender, the nipples on her perky little breasts like hard little pebbles.

"You're going to do just fine," he said, cupping her breasts and flicking at her nipples with his thumbs. He felt his penis responding to the feel of her firm, young flesh, her hard nipples. . .

. . . and there was a knock on the door.

"Damn!" he snapped.

The knock came again.

"All right, get dressed, Kathy."

"Yes, sir."

As she started to get dressed, he went over to the bed, where his own clothes were.

The knock again.

"All right, Philip!" he snapped.

When both he and Kathy were dressed, he walked her to the door. When he opened it he found his black houseman, Philip, standing there.

"I'm sorry to bother you while you're working, sir," Philip said.

"Philip, take Miss Reese over to Big Milly and tell her I said to put her on the payroll."

"Thank you, Mr. Sharp."

"That's all right, Kathy. You earned it."

"Sir, Mr. Skinner is in the living room."

"I'll take care of him, Philip. Take Kathy out the back way."

"Yes, sir. This way, Miss."

Jason Sharp walked to the end of the upstairs hall with Philip and Kathy, and when they went down the back stairs, he went down the front.

Sharp was in his mid-forties, but he looked a good ten years younger. He stood six-three and weighed over two hundred pounds, but rather than looking muscular he looked. . .rangy. He was aware that many women considered him to be beautiful, and he thought that other men resented him for it. Men like Skinner, who was decidedly unattractive to women. If the man wasn't a fair hand with a gun, he wouldn't even have kept him around.

He strode into the living room and found Skinner standing at the window.

"What can I do for you, Skinner?"

"That last batch of men you had brought in, Sharp—they're possibly the worst I've ever seen."

"It is getting hard to find decent men."

Skinner appeared to be surprised that Sharp was agreeing with him.

"I've got another possible candidate, though," Sharp said, walking to a small writing desk. He picked up a piece of paper and said, "The name is Bellman, Wes Bellman. Ever hear of him?"

"No, can't say I have."

"He's reputed to have killed a dozen men. I don't have any names of his victims, but if there was anyone of any consequence I'm sure we'd know."

"Well, what makes you think he's any good?"

"I don't know that he's any good," Sharp said. "That's what you're going to have to find out."

"Me?"

"Well, you're always complaining about the men who are brought in here. Maybe it's time for you to bring someone in who *is* good with a gun. What do you say?"

"Sure," Skinner said. "I've been cooped up here too long, anyway. I'd like to get out for a while."

"Fine. We'll try to pinpoint his location and you can leave in the morning."

"Great. I appreciate this."

"No problem, Skinner. I'll let you know tonight

where you're going to have to go to find him."

"I'll see you tonight, then," Skinner said. "Thanks, Sharp."

As Skinner started for the front door, Philip came into the room. Both men stopped and regarded each other with obvious distaste.

Skinner looked back at Sharp, wondering why the man would keep a nigger around—but then, that wasn't his problem. He didn't have to live in the same house with him.

He continued to the door without further word.

Philip entered the room and waited for Sharp to address him.

The black man was in his forties. His close-cropped hair was black, peppered with grey, and he moved slowly, deliberately, as if each move was carefully planned. He spoke the same way, as well.

"Did you get the girl taken care of?" Sharp asked.

"Yes, sir."

"Good."

Sharp reread the information he had on Wes Bellman, and then handed the sheet to Philip.

"I'm sending Skinner out after this one in the morning. See if we can't get a location on him."

"Skinner?"

"Yes. He's been bothering the other men too much lately with his whining. We need a break from him, and he needs a break from this place."

"Maybe he should be replaced."

"Maybe," Sharp agreed. Then, indicating the sheet of paper in Philip's hand, he said, "Maybe we have his replacement right there."

TEN

Wes Bellman was in San Pedro, New Mexico.

It had been six weeks since his reputation had been seeded throughout the Southwest. He'd been in New Mexico for five days, and had seen five towns. In each he'd been sure to make his presence known—mostly by using his mouth—and he was starting to think that he needed to do something drastic to make things happen.

San Pedro was a fair-sized town, and as such had its own newspaper, which was important. It was the first decent-size town he'd been in since he had crossed the border from Texas to New Mexico. If he did something noticeable in this town and it was in the newspaper, there was a possibility that it would be picked up by other newspapers.

He decided to do something that Clint Adams would never do. He was going to show off.

Skinner rode into San Pedro wondering if this time he would catch up with Bellman. The information he'd been given by Sharp had put him a couple of days behind Bellman instead of ahead of him, and he had the feeling that it had been deliberate. It meant that Sharp wanted him out of Lost City for a while.

Skinner wondered why.

Maybe he felt that Skinner was becoming too powerful in Lost City. Maybe he could take over from Sharp.
How about that?

Clint waited until the saloon was good and crowded
before going inside. He was careful to act as if he'd
already had a few beers too many at the town's other
saloon. In fact, he had put in an appearance at the other
saloon and swilled down a couple of beers just to be on
the safe side.

He walked to the bar and looked for two things: One,
the saloon girl who was getting the most attention. Two,
the man with the biggest opinion of himself.

The girl was easy to spot. A tall, buxom gal with hair
as black as a raven's wing. Her skin was firm and pale,
her legs long and graceful. She didn't belong in a town
like this, and it was only natural that she was the center
of attention.

The man took a little longer and, in fact, came in
after Clint. He was a big man with broad shoulders and
long arms. From the way he walked, you knew he had
confidence in his physical ability—but Clint could also
tell by the way he wore his gun that he could use that,
too.

He waited and watched, knowing that eventually the
two would gravitate together.

If it turned out that the women liked the man's atten-
tions, he was going to have to find another way to get
his attention. He wanted to pick a fight with the man,
but he didn't want it to go as far as it could.

He had two beers before the girl came over to him
during a circuit of the room. Two of the other girls had
tried for him, but he had turned them down flat.

"I'm waiting for Midnight," he'd said.

Apparently, it had gotten back to her.

"You the one calling me Midnight?"

"Yeah."

"They looked each other up and down.

"Why?"

"Why what?"

"Why are you calling me Midnight?"

"Come on," he said. "It fits, you know that."

"Nobody's ever called me that before."

"Nobody's been that smart, I guess."

"I guess not." She turned to the bartender and said, "Give this man—" She looked at Clint questioningly.

"Bellman, Wes Bellman."

"Give Mr. Bellman a beer on me."

"Thanks."

She looked him in the eyes and said, "Don't go away."

"I won't."

She continued on, then, and finally got to the table where the man was sitting with his two friends.

Clint watched carefully and had the feeling that the big man and woman knew each other—or had known each other in the past.

She moved around the room again and came back to him. He got the impression that she was trying to make a decision.

"That the same beer?"

"Same one," Clint said.

"You nursing it?"

He shrugged.

"Just seems to taste better than any of the others," he said, looking into the mug. "I don't know what it is. It just tastes. . .sweeter."

She stroked his cheek and kept on walking, but he

saw the big man looking their way—and he didn't look happy.

When she reached him, the man grabbed her by the arm and held her roughly. They exchanged a few words and then she tried to pull away, but she couldn't break his hold.

"It's time," Wes Bellman muttered and moved away from the bar.

He reached the table just as the man was saying, ". . . bitch, Sharon."

"And you're an animal, Tuck. Now let go of my arm."

"Not until you tell me you ain't forgot who you leave here with tonight."

"I'll leave with who I want. . .if I leave with anyone at all. Now let go!"

She pulled again, but the man was too strong for her. Their confrontation became the center of attention in the saloon and silenced all of the customary noise.

Everyone heard Wes Bellman speak.

"Let the lady go," Clint said.

All eyes turned to the bearded man, and the last set of eyes to look at him were the big man's.

"You talking to me?"

"You're the one holding the lady's arm."

"And I'm keeping it," the man said. "It's mine."

"Like hell!" Sharon said.

"What's your name, friend?" Clint asked.

"Tucker."

"I'm Bellman."

"So?"

"I'm telling you to let go of the lady's arm."

"And if I don't?"

"Well, I've told you my name," Clint said. "so you'll

know who broke your arm. . .if you don't.''

The big man became incensed by the threat—so incensed that he released Sharon and stood up, knocking his chair over.

"You better be able to use that gun, friend," Tucker said.

"This gun?" Clint asked, glancing down at the Navy Colt. "I can use this gun much better than you could ever use any gun, Tucker."

"Is that a fact?"

"Believe me, it is."

"You ready to prove it?"

"I don't want to kill you."

Tucker looked at his friends and said derisively, "The mountain man here doesn't want to kill me." He looked back at Clint and asked, "How do you suggest we settle this, then?"

"Why don't you just take your friends and leave?"

Tucker laughed at that, but before they could take the discussion any further, the batwing doors opened and a man wearing a badge walked in.

"What's going on?"

He was a tall man with an impressive belly, but there was nothing soft about it, or about him. He pushed his way to the point where Wes Bellman and Tucker were facing each other. He was at least as tall as Tucker and some thirty pounds heavier.

"You picking another fight, Tucker? You know, if you kill another man in this town—"

"It's all right, Sheriff," Clint said. "He's not going to kill anyone."

"Look, friend, I don't know who you are or what you want, but why don't you just turn around and walk out."

"My name's Bellman, Wes Bellman. Maybe you've heard of me?"

"No, I can't say that I have. Listen—"

"What's your name?"

"I'm Sheriff Patrick. Look, I'm telling you, the best thing for you to do is just leave—"

"I can't."

"Why not?"

"He insulted the lady."

The lawman looked at the three of them—Bellman, Tucker and Sharon—and said, "Sharon? Mister, these two are always insulting each other—"

"Not in my presence."

"Friend—"

"Just let us settle it, Sheriff," Tucker suggested. "Out in the street."

Clint could see that the lawman was wavering.

"Sheriff, I believe we can settle this right here."

"I don't want my place broken up!" the bartender shouted.

"Nothing will get broken," Clint said, "except maybe a few bottles, or some poker chips."

"What are you driving at?" the sheriff asked.

"Well, I believe I can convince Mr. Tucker here that he doesn't want to draw his gun against me."

"How do you intend to do that?"

"I'm kind of curious about that myself," Tucker said.

Clint looked at Tucker and thought, well that's good.

ELEVEN

Trick shooting was something that Clint Adams, the Gunsmith, loathed.

He hated people who had to show off with a gun. Most of them were not as good as they thought, anyway, and the ones who were accurate would never have been able to stand up against another man with a gun. Shooting plates and bottles was more their style.

After Clint explained his ideas to the sheriff and Tucker, he was somewhat surprised—and pleasantly so —that Tucker agreed.

"If you outshoot me," Clint said to Tucker, "I'll leave town."

"That's not good enough."

"What do you want, Tuck? He's offering you a way out without killing anybody."

"If I outshoot him I want him to *crawl* out of here, and out of town. . .on his belly."

"You can't ask a man to do—" the Sheriff started to say.

"I agree," Clint said, cutting the lawman off.

"You what?"

"I agree."

"Jesus."

They cleared out the center of the saloon and set up two tables at the far end. On each of the two tables they set up three empty long-necked bottles, with a shot glass balanced on the mouth of each.

"You've got to hit the glasses without knocking over or breaking the bottles," Clint said. "Do you understand?"

"Sure," Tucker said, but Clint thought he could see doubt in the man's eyes.

They stood at the other end of the floor, the wall on either side of them lined with men eagerly watching.

"Sheriff, you call it."

Clint's only doubt was about the Navy Colt. He hadn't used it for this kind of pinpoint firing yet.

But it was too late to think about that now.

"Are you both ready?" Sheriff Patrick asked.

Clint said "Yes," and Tucker only nodded. Off to his left, Clint could see Sharon watching, an eager look on her face. He thought briefly that winning here might have more pleasant results than he had originally thought.

She really was quite lovely.

"All right. . ." the Sheriff said, ". . .on the count of three: One. . .two. . .three."

The gasp of the crowd went up almost as one.

Wes Bellman's hand streaked for his gun and drew it before anyone could actually see him do it. He fired—not three times, but six.

He knocked the shot glasses off his bottles without so much as vibrating them. . .

. . .and then he shattered Tucker's three before the big man could even fire!

"Jesus Christ!" the Sheriff gasped.

Tucker looked at Clint wide-eyed, his gun in his left

hand. He had cleared leather, but just barely.

"Bellman wins," the Sheriff said, unnecessarily.

"Like hell. . ." Tucker said, and he turned and hit Clint in the face with his left fist, his right hand still holding his unfired gun.

"Tucker!" the Sheriff called out.

Tucker turned and saw the lawman holding his gun on him.

"Put up your gun."

"I don't need my gun," Tucker said, leathering it. "I'm gonna prove to mountain man here that he doesn't want to tangle with me man to man. If he beats me, *I'll* crawl out of town on my belly."

He glared down at Clint, who had blood in his beard from his nose.

"Bellman?" the Sheriff asked.

"I agree," Clint said from the floor, and Tucker sprang forward to stomp him.

As Tucker lifted his big boot Clint rolled to the side, and a group of men scattered to get out of his way. Tucker's boot came down on the floor with a loud bang, and he turned to find out where Clint had gone.

Clint had gained his feet and was watching Tucker warily. The man had huge arms, and he knew that what he wanted most was to wrap them around Clint and squeeze the life out of him. Clint had to avoid that at all costs.

Tucker shuffled toward Clint, who was content to wait for the big man to make the next move. Suddenly, faster than a man his size should have been, Tucker sprang forward—but Clint was ready. He extended his left in a powerful jab that caught the man on the nose. The blow stopped Tucker, staggered him a step, and brought tears to his eyes and blood to his nose.

Both men had now tasted their own blood, and neither one liked it.

Clint caught a look at Sharon over Tucker's shoulder. God she was breathtaking. Her nostrils were flaring as her breath came hard and she was licking her full lips in anticipation.

Amazingly, he found that he had a rock-hard erection.

"Come on," he said, his lust for the woman causing his patience to wear thin, "come on. . . ."

"I'm coming," Tucker said, "don't you worry. . . ."

Tucker came forward now, shoulders hunched, fists up, and Clint wondered if the man had ever done any time in a prize-fighting ring.

He jabbed again and caught Tucker on the chin, but the big man had a chin like granite.

Warily, they circled each other. Once Tucker feinted with his right and hit Clint in his ribs with his left. It felt like his whole side had caved in.

Tucker was strong!

After a few moments, Clint decided it was going on too long. He had hoped that the trick shooting would put an end to it, and he wasn't all that sure that he could beat Tucker man to man.

Clint began to back up, drawing Tucker with him. Behind him he heard men scramble out of the way, and eventually he was standing with his back to the wall.

"Got you now. . . ." Tucker said.

"Come and get it," Clint said.

Tucker moved forward and launched a right-handed punch that, if it had landed, probably would have driven Clint's head through the wall. At the last moment, Clint moved his head to the side and Tucker's fist struck the wall, causing cracks to stretch out in every direction from the point of impact.

The man bellowed in pain, but Clint did not wait for the cry to fade away. He ducked low and threw two hard punches to Tucker's midsection. As each blow hit he heard the man grunt. Tucker took two steps back, trying to flex the fingers of his right hand.

Clint threw what he hoped would be the finishing blow.

He launched a kick and caught Tucker right between the legs, driving his testicles up into his crotch. The big man's eyes popped and he opened his mouth to scream, but no sound came out.

Everyone watched as the big man stood paralyzed, and they were waiting for Clint to throw a punch to finish it.

But it was all over.

After Tucker's friends had picked him up and helped him out, the Sheriff came over to Clint.

"They're taking him to the doc's," he said. "You might have broke something."

"I hope not."

Clint held a cloth to his bloody nose, but the bleeding had already stopped.

"Are you really going to make him crawl out of town on his belly?"

"Would he have made me?"

"You're damn right he would have."

"Well, tell him he can walk. . .if he can."

"I'll tell him," the Sheriff said.

At that point, Sharon came over to Clint carrying a shot of whiskey.

The Sheriff looked at Clint and said, "Good luck, Bellman."

As the lawman walked away, Sharon handed Clint the whiskey.

"What did he mean by that?" Clint asked.

She smiled and said, "I've been known to break a man's. . .spirit."

He tossed off the whiskey and said, "Not this man, Midnight."

"We'll find out, cowboy," she said, stroking his cheek, "later."

"Is this going to be my reward?"

"Oh, yeah."

"Good," he said, "I thought I was going to have to pay for it."

"You already have, honey."

TWELVE

Standing in a corner of the saloon was a man who had watched all the proceedings with intense interest. Now he left his position and approached Wes Bellman, who had taken a table once they had all been restored to their original positions.

"Mind if I sit down?"

"You buying?"

"Sure."

"Be my guest."

"My name's Skinner," the man said, taking a seat directly opposite him.

"Bellman."

"I know."

They called one of the other girls over and Skinner ordered a bottle and two glasses.

"I was impressed."

"I wasn't," Clint said, gingerly feeling his nose. He was gratified to find that it wasn't broken.

"I don't mean with the fight," Skinner said. "You kind of won that fighting dirty, didn't you?"

"The point is to win."

"I guess it is. I was talking about your gunplay, though. I was very impressed."

"Just some trick shooting."

"But you were fast."

"He was slow."

"Maybe it was a combination of both."

"Maybe."

At that point the girl came with the bottle and they poured themselves a drink.

And then they poured another.

By the time the bottle was empty, they were very good buddies.

"Hey, Bellman?"

"Yeah?"

"Did you ever hear of something called the Fast Draw League?"

"The what."

"The F-fast Draw League."

"I think so. Some kind of—of a club, ain't it?"

"It's a club, all right. The kind of club that could use a man like—like you."

"Me? What for? I heard they were a bunch of—of amateurs."

"Well. . .we ain't."

"We?"

"That's right. I'm a member of the Fast Draw League —and from what I just saw, you should be, too."

"Why?"

"Because we could use you."

"As what?"

"Well. . .I can't tell you that, now."

"Why not?"

"I'm not—I don't have the authority to."

"Who does?"

"The man in charge."

"And who's that?"

"I can't tell you that."

"Why not?"

"Because I don't have—"

"—the authority. What do you suggest, then?"

"Take a ride with me tomorrow."

"Where?"

"To meet the man in charge. Listen to what he has to say, and then decide."

"Is he going to ask me to kill somebody?"

"He might."

"In that case, I'll take that ride."

"Good. Why don't we get another bottle."

"Yes, why don't we?"

"I'm finished here."

Clint looked up and saw Sharon standing next to him, a wrap around her shoulders.

"Would you like to walk me home?"

"Of course."

"What about your friend?"

He looked at Skinner, whose head was down on the table. He thought he could hear the man snoring lightly.

"Somebody else can walk him home," Clint said, standing up. "Come on."

As they left, Sharon asked, "Why aren't you as drunk as your friend?"

"I didn't drink as much as he did."

"Why not?"

"I had something else to look forward to, tonight," he said. "I didn't want to dull my senses."

THIRTEEN

The next morning Clint awoke with Sharon's raven tresses between his legs.

"What are you doing, woman?"

"Waking you," she said, looking up at him. "You said you wanted to get up at first light."

"Do you always get up this early?"

"I don't sleep much," she said. "A few hours is all I need."

"So I gather."

She had been damned near insatiable the night before—a result of having had two men fight over her, no doubt. She hadn't broken his spirit, but she damned near broke a few of his bones.

"I suspect you're leaving town this morning," she said. "Am I right?"

"Yes."

"Well, then," she said, grabbing hold of his stiff penis with both hands, "I'll have to give you a good send off, won't I?"

Her mouth descended on him, and as her head began to bob rhythmically, he said, "Only . . . if . . . you . . . insist!"

Later, Clint—wondering if Skinner would even re-

71

member—went to the livery stable where they were supposed to meet.

To his surprise, the man was there, waiting.

"Good morning, Bellman."

" 'Morning," Clint said.

"You look surprised."

"To tell you the truth, I am. I wasn't quite sure you'd make it this early."

"Why not?"

"You weren't exactly in great shape last night when we. . .parted company."

"You mean, when you left with that black-haired saloon girl?"

"You noticed that, huh?"

"I noticed her, and I noticed when you left."

"Then I guess you weren't as drunk as you appeared."

Skinner smiled, leaned forward and said, "Were you?"

"Maybe not."

"Well, now that we're both obviously sober," Skinner said, "have you changed your mind?"

"About taking that ride with you? No, I haven't. Where's the harm in taking a ride?"

"There's something else about this ride I should tell you."

"What?"

"You'll have to take the last part of it while blindfolded."

"Blindfolded?"

"The reason for that is if you refuse the offer you hear, I can lead you out again, and you won't be able to tell anyone where we're located."

"Let me get this straight," Clint said. "We're talking

about hiring my gun, right?''

"In one way or another, yeah, that's what we're talking about."

"It doesn't come cheap, you know."

"The League pays fairly well, Bellman."

"Well, in that case, let's get started."

They saddled their horses and mounted up, and Skinner led the way out of town, riding north.

Contact, Clint thought.

FOURTEEN

"This is crazy, Sandy."

The speaker was a red-haired young woman in her mid-twenties, with an extremely sensuous face and a very shapely body. Her lips were full, her eyes green, and her dark eyebrows contributed mightily to her appearance.

Her name was Anne Archer.

She was speaking to her partner, a tall, full-bodied blonde woman of about thirty, with shoulder-length hair the color of wheat, and blue eyes. While she was an extremely handsome woman, she was not the sensuous beauty that Anne Archer was.

Her name was Sandy Spillane.

There was also a third woman present, who was partners with the other two. She was a stunning, dark-haired girl, tall—though not as tall as Sandy Spillane—with full breasts and long legs. She was half Comanche, older than Anne, but younger than Sandy.

Her name was Katy Little Flower.

All three women were bounty hunters.

Sandy Spillane responded to Anne Archer's words.

"It's not crazy, Anne. You and Kathy go ahead and find what's his name."

"Dale Jameson," Katy said.

"Whoever. He's worth too much for us to give him up."

"I'm not saying that we should give him up, Sandy," Anne said. "Just that you should let us go with you. We can always find Jameson after we've found your brother."

"He's *my* brother, Anne, not yours and not Katy's. I'll find him, you find Jameson."

Anne looked at Katy, who shook her head. Both women knew that, of the three of them, Sandy was easily the most stubborn.

"All right, Sandy," Anne finally said. "Just do us a favor, will you?"

"What's that?"

"Be careful. We've all heard the rumors about the Fast Draw League."

"I'm always careful, girls," Sandy said. "You both know that."

Anna gaped at her friend and partner and said, "Are we talking about the same Sandy Spillane? The one who wanted to go after Bill Wallmann alone?"

"But I didn't, did I? We got the Gunsmith to go with us. That was your idea, Anne, and I agreed."

Anne Archer felt a pang of remorse at the thought of Clint Adams. The only man she'd ever really cared for, and she had let him get away.

"All right, don't start moping again," Sandy said to Anne.

"I'm not moping," Anne said, defensively. "I'm worrying."

"Already? I haven't even left."

They were sitting in a saloon in the town of Canton, Colorado, a beer mug in front of each of them.

"When we're finished with these beers, I suggest we

get going,'' Katy Little Flower said. She had taken a couple of sips from hers, and as far as she was concerned she was finished. She didn't like beer, but she admitted that it cut dust better than anything else she'd ever tried.

Outside the saloon, the three bounty hunters said their farewells.

"Sandy, remember you promised to be careful. Don't go charging in with your gun blazing or anything," Anne Archer warned.

"Give me credit for having a little more tact than that, Annie.''

"Don't call me Annie!"

Sandy laughed, and then her partners began laughing with her.

"Watch out for her, Katy, and for yourself.''

"You, too.''

Sandy hugged each of her partners in turn and then mounted up.

"Nick's message said that he was somewhere around San Pedro,'' Sandy said. "That's where I'll start.''

"We'll be in South Texas," Anne said. "If you need us, just send a wide message. It'll get to us.''

"Just get Jameson," Sandy said. "He's worth five hundred dollars apiece to us.''

She wheeled her horse around and rode toward New Mexico, while her partners headed for Texas.

"We shouldn't let her go alone," Anne said.

"We need the money from Jameson," Katy pointed out.

"I know," Anne said, staring after their friend. "I know. Let's get going. . . .''

•　　•　　•

Thinking about the group called the Fast Draw League—a group possibly made up of gunmen and killers—Sandy Spillane wondered aloud, "Where is the Gunsmith when I need him?"

"All right," Skinner said, calling a halt to their progress. "From this point on I'll have to blindfold you, before we get to Lost City."

"Lost City?"

"That's what we call it—and I can tell you the name of the town because it isn't on any map."

Skinner maneuvered his way around behind Clint to blindfold him.

For the first time, Clint truly missed Duke. The big gelding would be able to find his way in and out of Lost City after traveling the route once. Also, Duke would make sure that no harm came to him while he was blindfolded.

For the moment, Clint Adams was truly in the dark.

FIFTEEN

When the knock came on Jason Sharp's bedroom
door this time, he and the woman he was with were
finished.

"Come in."

Philip entered and walked to the foot of the bed. On
it, both Sharp and the woman—a bountiful brunette
named Carlotta—were naked. Carlotta's breasts were
large and pendulous, with large, brown nipples, but
Philip seemed scarely to notice.

"Skinner is riding in, sir."

"He's back already?"

"Yes, sir."

"Alone?"

"No. He's got someone with him, blindfolded."

"He must have found Bellman."

Sharp stood up and stretched. The girl reached for his
semi-erect penis, but he slapped her hand away.

"That's all for today, Carlotta," he told her. Then he
looked at Philip and said, "Unless Philip has some use
for you?"

The girl gave the black man a coquettish look that he
pointedly ignored.

"No, sir. I don't have any need for her."

"Get dressed, Carlotta, and go out the back way."

"Whatever you say, Jason."

Getting dressed, Sharp looked at Philip and said, "Sometimes I wonder about you, Philip."

"It's a waste of your time to think about me, sir."

"I guess. All right, that's all. Have someone show Skinner and Bellman into my office in the saloon. I'll see them there."

"Yes, sir."

Sharp turned and caught Carlotta as she was bending over to put on her pants. Her pendulous breasts hung and swayed, gently slapping against each other. There were times when he loved breasts like that, and then there were other times when he preferred small, firm breasts, the kind that barely moved.

The truth was that he loved all women, big and small, and they took up a lot of his time, but there was time enough for that later. Now it was time for business, and as much as he liked women and sex, business came first.

He finished dressing and saw Carlotta to the back stairs.

"When will I see you again?" she asked.

He slapped her, a hard stinging slap that rocked her head and left her cheek red.

"Do you want to?"

Rubbing her cheek, fighting the tears that stung her eyes, she said, "Y-yes."

"Well, maybe sometime soon," he said. He tapped her lightly on the same cheek, and then she smiled and kissed his hand.

"Get out of here."

As she went down the back steps, he descended the front. He went to the office he maintained in the house and took his gun and shoulder holster out of his desk.

Once he had slipped into it, he grabbed a jacket and put it on.

"All right, Skinner," he said. "Let's see what you've brought us."

When Johnny Skinner came riding in with the blindfolded man, there were several Fast Draw League members on the street. One in particular, Len Tobey, stared at the two men with great interest.

"What's wrong, Len?" his friend, Bill Evans, asked.

"That man, the one coming in with Skinner. . . ."

"What about him?"

"I think I know him. . . ."

"Who is he?"

"When the blindfold comes off I'll know better. Come on," he said, grabbing his friend's arm, "let's go across the street so I can get a better look."

When Skinner removed the blindfold, Wes Bellman blinked his eyes against the high flying sun and found himself in front of a saloon.

"What's this?"

"The Lost City Saloon."

Clint looked around, up and down the street of Lost City, and thought that it looked more like a ghost town. He said as much.

"That's what it was before we took it over."

"How many people live here?"

"Not many. There's thirty League members right now, and about five or six shop owners. Then there's Big Milly and her girls."

"Big Milly?"

"Yeah. She runs the whorehouse."

"I think I could have guessed that."

"Actually, she runs it for Sharp."

"Who's Sharp?" Clint asked, even though the name struck a sudden cord.

"He's the man who runs the League," Skinner said, and then added, "for now."

Clint filed the remark away for future reference. Apparently, Skinner had ambitions.

"This place have the usual? General store, hardware, gunshop, bank, telegraph—"

"Some of them. You'll find out all about that—if you stay."

"Where do we go from here?"

"Inside, for a drink."

"When do I meet the man?"

"Inside," Skinner said, "after the drink."

"Well, let's go, then. We leave the horses here?"

Skinner pointed to a man who was walking over and said, "He'll take care of the horses. That's his job."

"Why don't we take them over to the livery?"

Skinner said, "That's his job," again, and Clint shrugged and dismounted.

As the blindfold came off the stranger, Len Tobey caught his breath.

"It's him!"

"Who?" Evans asked. "It's who?"

"His name's Tom Sideman," Len Tobey said, "and five years ago he killed my brother. I always knew I'd find him, someday."

Tobey started forward and Evans grabbed his arm.

"Wait a minute, Len. It's been five years. What if you're wrong?"

"I'm not," Tobey said, pulling his arm free.

"Lenny, give it some more time," Evans said. "It's been five years already, and he's not going anywhere. Be dead sure before you make a move."

"I'm sure," Tobey said, backing off in deference to his friend, "but he's the one who's gonna be dead. . . ."

Clint followed Skinner into the saloon, which was empty except for the bartender and a saloon girl, who bore no resemblance at all to Sharon. This one was thin, with dull blonde hair and a bored expression that changed only slightly when Skinner and Clint entered.

"Hello, Rita."

"Hi, Skinner. Who's your friend?"

"I'll introduce you later," Skinner said, "if he decides to stay."

As they walked to the bar, Skinner said, "She's not much to look at, but she can use her mouth for more than talking, boy, let me tell you."

"I'll take your word for it."

"Delaney, two beers."

"Comin' up."

The bartender was in his fifties, a medium-sized man with extremely powerful forearms. He was also wearing a sidearm, a Navy Colt almost identical to the one Clint was wearing, except that it was not as well cared for.

"I see you're wearing a Navy Colt," Clint said. "You like it?"

"A gun's a gun, friend," Delaney said, putting two beers on the bar. "Somebody didn't pay their bill one night, so I took this. It'll do until somebody else doesn't pay their bill."

"Drink up, Bellman," Skinner said, picking up his beer. "I'll check and see if Sharp is ready to see you."

"Does he know we're here?"

"Believe me," Skinner said, "he knows."

Skinner took his beer and walked to the back of the saloon, where he went through a beaded doorway.

"You joinin' up?" Delaney asked, leaning his impressive forearms on the bar.

Clint sipped his beer, wiped away the foam with the back of his hand and asked, "Is that up to me?"

"No, it ain't."

"Then I guess I don't know, do I?"

The man shrugged and said, "I was just making conversation."

"Well, make it someplace else."

As the bartender walked away, Clint felt a hand touch his elbow. It was Rita, the saloon girl.

"You don't like talking?"

"I pick who I talk to."

"How about talking to me?"

"Why not? Want a drink?"

"Naw. What's your name?"

"Bellman."

"Just Bellman? No first name?"

"Wes."

"Wes Bellman."

"That's the name."

"I never heard of you. What makes you think the League will take you in?"

"It wasn't my idea to try," he said, "so I guess I don't much care one way or the other if they do."

"What did you do that impressed Skinner enough for him to bring you here?"

"Not much."

"Well, it's true that it doesn't take much to impress Skinner—"

At that point Skinner stepped through the beaded curtain again.

"Hey, Bellman. The man is ready."

Clint looked at Rita and said, "I'm being called into the presence."

"He'll try to stare you down," she said in a low voice. "If he can't, you're in."

"Tell me something."

"What?"

"What's Sharp's first name?"

"Jason."

That's what I was afraid of, he thought.

He pinched her on the hip and said, "Thanks."

"See you."

Clint carried his beer to the beaded curtain, beyond which he would meet the man in charge of the Fast Draw League.

SIXTEEN

"Bellman, this is Jason Sharp," Skinner said. "Mr. Sharp, this is the man I told you about—Wes Bellman."

"Mr. Bellman," Sharp said from behind his desk. "Skinner has told me a lot about you."

"He hasn't told me a whole hell of a lot about you."

"That will come in time," Sharp said. "If you decide to stay with us."

"As I understand it, first you have to decide that you want me."

"Well, that's what we're here for, isn't it? Have a seat, please."

Clint sat down opposite Sharp, still holding his beer.

"A drink?" Sharp asked.

"I'm fine."

"A cigar, then?"

"Sure."

Sharp opened a box on his desk and Clint leaned forward to take a cigar.

He guessed that Sharp did this with everyone, so that he could get a good close look at their faces. In this case, however, his was a face that the man had seen before, and if Sharp recognized it, he'd be in a lot of trouble.

He was fairly sure his disguise would hold up, though, because he might not have recognized Jason

Sharp if he hadn't heard his name beforehand. When Clint had last seen him, twenty years ago, he had been a tall, gangly deputy sheriff. He'd had no confidence in himself at all, even though he'd been able to attract women even then. Now, Clint figured he drew the women like flies to honey. He had filled out, growing into his height, and now he was the self-assured leader of a band of killers.

Jason, how the hell did you come to be here?

Clint took his time choosing a cigar, giving Sharp ample time to look him over. At one point, as Rita had warned, Sharp's eyes caught him and held. Clint leaned back, lighting the cigar with a lucifer he'd taken from the same box, and he stared straight into Sharp's eyes. Next to him, he could feel Skinner shifting from one foot to the other.

"How long does this go on?" he asked.

"Skinner tells me you want to join us," Sharp said, ignoring the remark.

"He can't have told you that."

"Oh? Why not?"

"Because he's the one who told me that the League could use a man like me. I never brought it up."

"Well, would you like to join us?"

"As I understand it, that's not really up to me."

"No, it's not."

"So where do we go from here?"

"Skinner tells me you're very good with a gun."

"Skinner's right."

"Would you be willing to put on a demonstration for me? With your gun?"

"Sure. When?"

"Tomorrow morning."

"Why not today?"

"I have other business matters to attend to today."

Clint shrugged and said, "All right. What do I do in the meantime? You mind if I take a look around?"

"No, of course not. In fact, I'll have Skinner show you around—won't you, Skinner?"

"Sure."

"Maybe he'll even show you Big Milly's. I'm sure you'd like that."

Clint Adams would have passed, but Wes Bellman said, "I sure would."

"All right, then. I'll see you in the morning."

Sharp made no move to rise or shake hands, but Clint knew his audience was over.

He stood up and looked at Skinner expectantly.

"Skinner will be along in a moment, Bellman. I have some other business to discuss with him."

"Okay. I'll wait outside and talk to Rita."

"You do that."

After Clint had left, Skinner had to wait while Sharp lit a cigar and got it going to his satisfaction.

"Well? What do you think?"

"He's a good man with a gun," Skinner said, "and with his hands, too."

"Is that a fact? Tell me something: is he a killer?"

"I can't say as I ever saw him kill anybody, but yeah, I'd say he is."

"Well, answer me this, then," Sharp said. "If he's a killer, and he's so damned good with a gun, how come we never heard of him up to now. . .hmm?"

SEVENTEEN

Clint got another beer from the bar and walked over to where Rita was sitting.

"What are you doing here?" he asked her.

"I work here."

"No, I mean how did you come to be here, in this town?"

"You mean you want my life story? Are you trying to make friends so I'll talk to you about other things?"

"You're right."

"You want information."

"Right again."

"About Jason?"

"You're never wrong, are you?"

She laughed and said, "Remind me to tell you about that, sometime."

"Are you Sharp's woman?"

She laughed again.

"I ain't never even seen the inside of his house. No, he hasn't got around to me, yet. There's a lot of other women in town he still has to plow his way through."

"How long has he been here?"

"A long time."

"As head of the League?"

"He started it, if that's what you mean."

"Does he—"

"Talking about Sharp is a real unhealthy thing to do, Mister Bellman."

"Wes."

"Oh yeah, Wes," she said, grinning. "We're friends, right?"

"I'd like to be."

She hesitated, and then Skinner came through the curtained doorway.

"Let me think about it," she said quickly.

Skinner came over and said, "Come on, Bellman. I'll show you where you bunk."

"Nice talking to you, Rita."

As he walked outside with Skinner the man said, "You were *talking* to her?"

"Sure, why not?"

"Nobody ever talks to Rita. You just drop your pants and let her do all the talking."

"Sharp, too?"

"Jason don't bother with her."

They stepped off the boardwalk and started across the street.

"You two talk about me while I was gone?"

"Sure."

"What did you say?"

"I told him we could use you."

"And what'd he say?"

"He said we'd see."

"That's all?"

Skinner stopped walking and looked at Clint.

"That's all I'm ready to say right now, Bellman. After tomorrow, that may change."

"So I guess a lot is riding on how well I do tomorrow, huh?"

"I guess," Skinner said, "but I'm hitching my wagon to your team, Bellman. I just want you to know that."

"I appreciate the vote of confidence."

"Yeah," Skinner said. "Come on, stop asking questions for now and I'll show you where to put your gear."

"Okay," Clint said, "no more questions . . . for now."

EIGHTEEN

Skinner showed Clint to a room on the second floor of the Lost City Hotel. There was no desk clerk—you just grabbed a key and a room, Skinner explained.

"Your gear is already inside," Skinner said in the hall outside of Clint's room.

"Are all the rest of these rooms occupied?"

"Some are, some aren't. Most of us who work for Sharp room in the boardinghouse at the other end of town. Sometimes we just use these rooms for an evening's fun—if you know what I mean."

"Big Milly doesn't supply rooms?"

"If you use Big Milly's girls, and her rooms, then it costs you money."

"You mean there are other available women in town?"

"Some."

"Members of the League?"

"You never knew any women who could use a gun?"

"One or two."

"Well, there's one or two here, then there's Rita, and a couple of girls from the cafe, one who cleans at the boardinghouse—"

He stopped and laughed.

"What's so funny?"

"Betty, the gal who cleans our place. She's got to be careful somebody's not in a room that she goes in to clean, otherwise she don't get out for a while."

"Can't she say no?"

"That one? Hell, she don't want to. She loves it. That's why she took that job."

"Maybe I'll get to meet her."

"Maybe, if you stay around. Once you're a member, you'll get a room over there."

"How much do *you* have to say about whether or not I get accepted?"

"Quite a bit," Skinner said, and Clint felt he was lying. "It's really going to be up to you, though. If you impress Sharp tomorrow, then you'll be one of us. If you got any real flashy tricks, you better haul them out tomorrow."

"I'll try to dredge up a couple."

"Why don't you get some rest and I'll come back and get you in a couple of hours. I, uh, got some things to do, myself. You know?"

"Sure. Thanks, Skinner."

"Forget it. If I'm doing you a favor, you're gonna owe me one."

"I'll remember."

"I'll remind you."

As Skinner started away Clint called out, "Hey."

"What?"

"I could use a bath."

"Bath house is downstairs on the side, but you'll have to get your own water. Pump's outside."

After Skinner left, Clint went into his room and found his gear on the bed. He walked over to the window and watched Skinner walk down the street.

Okay, Cartwright, he thought, I'm here—but I don't

know where *here* is, and I don't know how to get word to you.

He decided he was really going to have to do some fancy shooting tomorrow to make sure he impressed Sharp. Once he was a member he might be able to find a telegraph line in town, or maybe get out of town to scout around and discover just where the hell Lost City was in New Mexico.

Lying down on the bed to get some much needed rest, he wondered where Jim West was and what he was doing just about now.

Sandy Spillane was tired.

She rode into the town of Lucky Touch, New Mexico, on a horse that was even more tired than she was.

"All right, girl," she said, patting the horse's lathered neck, "we'll get some rest here."

She found the livery stable and dismounted.

"What can I do for you, little lady?" the liveryman asked. He was five inches taller than Sandy, and liked what he saw. A *big* woman, just his type. Blonde, buxom, big in every way.

"Take good care of her."

"For how long?"

"I'd like to leave tomorrow."

"The way this horse is lathered up you should give her more time than that to rest. In fact, you look like you could use some rest, too."

"Just take care of the horse, mister. I'll take care of myself."

"Tough lady."

"Tougher than any you'll ever meet."

"I like tough ladies," he said, moving toward her, "especially big ones."

"Mister—"

"You must need a big man to satisfy you, honey," the man said. "Well, I'm Moose Callahan, the biggest, strongest man in town."

"Mister—"

"I'm gonna show you some pleasurin' you ain't never going to forget."

"Mister," she said, drawing her gun and pointing it at his nose.

"Whoa, hey, hold on there, lady—" His eyes crossed as he tried to train both of them on the barrel of the gun.

"I don't have the time or the inclination to play games with you. You take care of my horse—you take good care of my horse. You understand?"

The look in her eyes made him stop, and then take a step back.

"Okay, lady, okay."

"And that's all you'll take care of."

"That's my business," the man said. "I ain't never mistreated a horse in my life."

"See that you don't start now." She cocked the gun and added, "Understand?"

"All right, I understand. Put the gun up."

She eased the hammer down and backed away from him, keeping her gun in her hand.

"Tough bitch," he said again, admiringly.

She left the livery, confident that the man would care for the animal properly. He may have been a braggart, but he seemed sincere when he spoke of not mistreating horses.

She holstered her gun and started walking down the town's main street. She needed just one night's rest—she and the horse—and then she'd be on her way again.

But first, a drink.

Sandy knew the chance she was taking by entering the saloon. She'd already encountered one overly amorous Romeo in Lucky Touch, but she needed a drink to cut the dust, and she needed something more than the coffee she'd been able to get from a cafe.

She entered the saloon and approached the bar, aware that there were more than several sets of eyes watching her progress.

"Beer, please."

The bartender, looking amused, said, "Sure, little lady. My pleasure."

When he brought the beer he set it down and then leaned on the bar.

"Are you going to be in town long, honey?"

"Don't call me honey," she said, wrapping her left hand around the beer mug.

The bartender stood up to his full height, which was about four—maybe even five—inches more than her own.

"You're in *my* place, *honey*—that means I can call you what I want."

"Okay," she said, "if I can call you what I want."

"Sure, honey. What would you like to call me?"

She grinned at him and said, "Ugly."

The place erupted in laughter.

"Hey, listen—"

"I just came in here to have a beer," she said to the man. "Just let me have it in peace and I'll be on my way."

"Hey, you don't talk to me like that in my place—"

As she sipped her beer he grabbed her arm, gripping it tightly and painfully in one massive hand.

"Bitch!"

She spit a stream of beer out of her mouth and caught him squarely in the right eye.

"Hey!"

He released her arm and his hands flew to his face. They stopped short of their target, however, when he felt the barrel of Sandy's gun press beneath his chin.

"Hey," he said again, but with less conviction.

"Let me guess," she said. "Your name is. . . ."

"Bull."

"That figures. Your name is Bull and you are the strongest and biggest man in town, and you think I need a big man to satisfy me. Right?"

She pressed the barrel of her gun hard under his chin.

"Yeah, well—"

"You wouldn't be related to that big jerk at the livery stable, would you?"

Through the laughter she heard him say, "Uh, well yeah, he's my brother."

"That figures, too."

"Could you move that gun?" he said, straining his eyes to look down at it.

"I'll tell you what, Bull," she said, picking up her beer with left hand. "I'll just finish my beer this way, and when I'm done I'll move the gun. How does that strike you?"

"Fine," he said as she pressed harder, "just fine."

In a corner of the room, a man sat and watched the proceedings at the bar. The big blonde stood easily against the bar, beer in one hand and the gun in the other, and finished her beer in a leisurely manner.

The man was impressed.

He thought that she might make a good addition to the Fast Draw League.

The man's name was Gentry.

* * *

When he realized that if he wanted a bath it would have to be a *cold* bath, Clint opted for a simple pitcher and bowl. He cleaned up and got back to his room in time to put on a clean shirt and be ready for Skinner.

"Did you get your bath?"

"Almost," Clint said. "I'm refreshed enough. Where are we going now?"

"Sharp wants me to show you around town, so I'll show you around. Let's get started."

Outside Clint said, "Uh, what is there to see in Lost City?"

"Not a hell of a lot," Skinner said. "I just thought we'd start at Big Milly's."

"Well," Clint said, "that sounds like a good place to start."

NINETEEN

Big Milly was true to her name.

A woman in her late forties—or even her early fifties, if all the makeup was hiding a multitude of sins—she was shaped like a guernsey cow.

"Well, Skinner. You haven't been in here in a long time."

"I've been away, Big Milly."

"Hah! Not long enough."

Skinner thought she was kidding and laughed, but Clint detected a hint of truth in her voice.

"Who's this?"

"This is Bellman," Skinner said. "He's a new man. . .maybe."

"Welcome to Big Milly's," the woman said. She waved an arm and said, "Come into my parlor."

He looked into her parlor and saw about a half-dozen women in various stages of dress—or undress. There were all size, shapes and colors, all doing their best to look seductively sexy.

"Not bad, huh?" Skinner asked, nudging Clint.

"You said it," Clint lied.

In truth, Big Milly's stable was somewhat less than first class. At least two of the whores looked like they were forty or more, one of the others was on the heavy

103

side, with chunky thighs and breasts. The other three were the best of the lot, and of them, only one could really be called pretty. The other two were, at least, young.

"What do you want?" Big Milly asked.

"I'll take Lily, Milly."

"Lily," Big Milly called out.

To Clint's surprise, the girl with the chunky thighs and breasts came forward and slid her arm through Skinner's.

Apparently, Skinner liked meaty women.

"See you later, Bellman," Skinner said. "Don't hurt yourself."

"Have fun," Clint said.

"Well, Mr. Bellman? What's your pleasure?"

"Uh, Skinner didn't mention the price."

"Don't worry about the price, honey. Consider this a free sample. Once you sign on, then you can worry about the price."

Clint looked at the women in the room, wishing there was somebody of Sharon's caliber there. Milly mistook his reluctance as indecision.

"Let me pick out a good for you, son."

"Sure, Milly."

"Jackie."

One of the women who looked forty stood up and came over. She was wearing a filmy peignor through which he could see her solid breasts and brown nipples.

"Take this man upstairs and show him what he gets for his money if he joins the League."

"Sure, Milly," Jackie said. Her voice was deep and throaty, almost raspy. "Come on, lover."

He took his hand and led him up the stairs. From behind, he watched her rounded buttocks clench and unclench as they took the steps, and in spite of himself he started to react.

She was, after all, a half-naked woman of some merit. She smelled sweet and she didn't sag, and he didn't have any better way of passing the time.

She led him to a room, opened the door and just about pushed him in. Once inside she shed her peignor quickly and stood with her hands on her hips and her legs spread.

"Not bad, huh? For someone my age. Is that what you're thinking?"

Her breasts were round and firm, her thighs solid. Her belly was by no means flat, but there was nothing unattractive about the slight bulge there.

"Actually, I don't know your age, but I'd have to agree," he said. "Not bad at all."

"Well," she said, "let's get rid of those pants and see what you can do about it."

When he got downstairs, he found Skinner already waiting.

"Well?" the man asked.

"Well what?"

"How was it?"

"It was fine."

Actually, it was much more than fine. Jackie was a very experienced—if somewhat used—whore, and had not allowed his interest to stray even once.

"See what you're in for if you stay?"

"It's still not my decision."

"Sure it is," Skinner said. "If you want to stay bad enough, you'll impress the hell out of Sharp tomorrow."

"I guess I will, then."

"Good. Come on, we'll get a drink and meet some of the other boys."

"If you don't mind, Skinner," Clint said, "I'd rather get something to eat, and then go back to my room and rest up for tomorrow."

He looked upstairs to indicate what he had to rest up from.

"I'd also like to clean my gun and make sure it works fine, tomorrow."

"Good thinking. All right, it's a little early for me to be eating, I always eat late, but I'll take you to the cafe and leave you there. You can find your way back to your room from there."

"No problem. Thanks."

"Hey," Skinner said, slapping Clint on the back, "I want you in top shape tomorrow. I've got big plans for you, Bellman. Big plans."

"The Fast Draw what?" Sandy Spillane asked, feigning ignorance.

"The Fast Draw League. You must have heard of it."

"Can't say as I have, Mr. Gentry."

"Well, look—I'm sort of a scout for them, and I was impressed with what you did in there."

They were walking down the street away from the saloon, the man having followed her after she walked out.

"I had a beer."

"Come on, lady—"

"Spillane, Sandy Spillane."

"Can I call you Sandy?"

"Why not? You're the only man I've met in this town so far that didn't want to put his hands on me."

"Don't count on it," he said, "but I'd have to get to know you a little better before I tried."

"That's still refreshing. Anyway, I didn't fast draw anybody. I just stuck my gun in some fool's face."

"You came out with that gun pretty quick after you spit that beer in his eye."

She shrugged.

"Maybe."

"No maybe about it. Look, let me tell you something about the League and you can decide for yourself if you're interested."

"You know a place around here to eat?"

"Sure."

"Okay. You can talk to me while I eat."

"Fine."

On the way to the cafe, Sandy tried to control the rapid beating of her heart. She did not want her anxiety to show.

She couldn't believe her luck at having made contact this way. Now all she had to do was not play too hard-to-get and blow it.

After dinner, Gentry walked Sandy to the hotel.

"Sorry," the desk clerk said, "but I just gave out the last room."

"Damn," Sandy said. "I should have come here first."

"Look, Pop, I'll give the lady my room."

"You don't have to—"

"It's only for one night, right? You are going to come with me tomorrow, aren't you?"

"Sure I am—"

"Then here, take the key," he said, digging it out of his pocket. "I'll bunk in the livery."

"You don't have to bunk in the livery, Gentry," she said, not leaving any doubt as to what she was saying.

She wanted to get close to this man before they got to the League, and luckily he wasn't half bad looking.

He swallowed and said, "You mean. . .you want to share the room with me?"

"Sure, why not?"

"And what about the bed?"

"That too," she said, poking him in the side with her finger. "After all, it's only for one night. . .right?"

TWENTY

Back in his room, Clint stretched out on the bed, hands clasped behind his head. He needed a sure-fire trick tomorrow to impress the hell out of Sharp.

Jason Sharp had to be wondering where a man like Wes Bellman had come from, and after he saw him shoot his curiosity would be uncontainable.

In addition to a good trick, he had to come up with a good explanation as to why his fame had not spread further and wider than it had to this point.

It took him the better part of an hour, but he finally thought he had come up with both.

Before drifting off to sleep, Clint thought briefly about Jason Sharp.

Sharp had been a deputy in the same town that Clint had been a deputy—where the hell was that? Damned if he could remember.

He remembered Sharp, though, because although they had never become friends, they had talked a lot—or rather, Sharp had talked and Clint had listened.

The gangly youth had expressed concern more than once about whether or not he would become somebody.

"You're good with a gun, Clint," he had said on more than one occasion, "real good. That gun is gonna make you somebody. What do I have?"

Clint had never been able to answer that question, because as far as he was concerned, the boy was right. He *did* have nothing to build on, not as long as he had absolutely no confidence in himself.

Sharp had never been able to figure out what to do with the attraction that he seemed to hold for women. The girls in town had just seemed to want to. . .mother him, while they never did anything motherly with Clint, at all.

Now, Jason Sharp was the head of the Fast Draw League.

Clint knew that people changed over the years—especially a span of twenty years—but for Jason Sharp to have changed this much, something must have happened to him.

As much as he wanted to get word out to Cartwright about where the League was located, he found himself wanting to find the answer to this dilemma.

What had changed Jason Sharp so much?

Jason Sharp sat in his office in the saloon, smoking another cigar. In half an hour he was to meet a girl called Jackie at his house. Jackie, he had found, though one of the older women at Big Milly's, was one of the most satisfying to him. She knew exactly how to please him, and still sought new ways to do so.

First, however, he had to make sure that nothing would interfere with his enjoyment of her.

He was thinking about the new man, Bellman. There had been something awfully familiar about him, but he couldn't put his finger on it. He had been thinking about it for several hours, but now he abruptly crushed out his cigar and stood up.

Enough about Bellman. Tomorrow he would test the man. If he passed, then he'd become part of the League—until he proved he couldn't be trusted.

If he failed to impress, then the same thing would happen to him that had happened to every other man who failed: He'd be killed on the spot.

TWENTY-ONE

Over breakfast at the cafe the following morning, Clint explained to Skinner what his plans were for a trick.

"Who you gonna get to help you with something as crazy as that?" Skinner asked.

Clint just stared at Skinner and smiled.

"Whoa, boy, let's not go off half-cocked on this."

"Correct me if I'm wrong, but you seem to have as much interest, maybe more, in my being accepted into the League."

"Well, yeah, I've got plans. . . ."

"So you'll be only too happy to help me out on this, right?"

"I don't know—"

"I'll even pay for breakfast."

Skinner looked down at his empty plate, then called the waitress over and said, "Bring me another breakfast, same thing as before."

"Is that a *yes*?" Clint asked.

Skinner made face and said, "Yeah."

Sharp rolled off of Jackie, but she held on and rolled over with him, ending up on top of him.

"Do we have some time to spend in bed this morning?" she asked hopefully.

"Not today, honey," he said. "I have a new man to look at today."

"Wes Bellman?"

"That's right. How did you know?"

"Skinner brought him to the house last night. Big Milly asked me to impress him."

"And did you?"

"I think so, but he was pretty impressive himself."

"Is that a fact?"

Jackie realized that she might have made a mistake and quickly tried to make up for it.

"Not as impressive as you, of course, but he was all right. Better than most of the drunken cowboys I have to deal with every day."

"What was your impression of him, Jackie?"

"What do you mean?"

"Well, you're probably one of the smartest women in town, certainly smarter than all of the whores at Big Milly's. What did you think of the man beyond his capabilities in bed?"

"Well, we didn't do too much talking, but my initial impression was that he wasn't too enthusiastic about being at Milly's."

"Anything else?"

"Well, he didn't bluster and brag the way most men do when they're in bed with you. I don't know, I guess he was kind of nice."

She wasn't sure if she had satisfied Sharp or not, but she didn't want to get Bellman in trouble, either. She had kind of liked him last night.

"Does that help?"

He pushed her off of him and said, "Not a whole hell of a lot."

He got up off the bed and now she was more worried

about getting herself in trouble than Bellman.

"Well, there is one more thing, but it was only a feeling I got."

Dressing, he said, "Tell me about it."

"Well, I just had the impression that he was trying to be someone he wasn't, you know? His personality just didn't seem to match his appearance—and when he *was* brash, it didn't seem to be something that came naturally."

Belting his pants Sharp was staring straight ahead at the window.

"Does that help?"

"It might," he said, "it just might."

Jackie breathed a sigh of relief.

Skinner took Clint over to the saloon, which at that time of the morning wasn't yet open.

"We going inside?" Clint asked.

Skinner shook his head.

"Out back. Sharp has sort of a firing range set up out there."

"Tell me something about Sharp."

"What?"

"How does he handle a gun?"

"Nobody knows."

"Nobody's ever seen him use one?"

Skinner shook his head.

"He wears a shoulder rig, but I've never seen him have to use his gun. I don't think anyone has."

"What qualifies him to head up the Fast Draw League, then?"

"It was his idea," Skinner said.

"That's fine, but how does he intend to keep his authority when—if—somebody tries to challenge it?"

"That's what I've been wondering about myself—more and more, lately."

"Nobody's tried to challenge him yet?"

"Not in the months I've been here. Sort of makes you think it's about time, huh?"

As they approached the saloon, they noticed two figures entering town on horseback and heading for the livery. Clint thought he recognized one of them.

"Who are those people?"

Skinner squinted in their direction and said, "The man is Gentry."

"And the woman?"

Skinner shrugged and said, "I don't know. Maybe she's a new whore for Milly's. That's about all Gentry is good for, recruiting new whores."

"That one doesn't look like a whore," Clint said. "She's wearing a gun."

"So she is. Come on, Sharp should be waiting."

Clint followed Skinner, throwing a last over the shoulder glance at the man and the big, blonde woman wearing the gun.

No, it couldn't be.

TWENTY-TWO

As it turned out, Sharp wasn't waiting for them; he made them wait for him.

"He's trying to make you nervous," Skinner said.

"I'm not nervous."

"Shit, I am."

This meant a lot to Skinner. He finally thought he had someone who could back him up in a takeover attempt against Sharp. If, however, Sharp sensed this, then nothing Bellman did would impress him.

"Does Sharp make this decision on his own?"

"No. There will be three other men here, all instructors."

"Gentry?"

"No. Gentry wasn't expected back today, so I'd say he won't be here."

The back door of the saloon opened and Jason Sharp stepped out.

"The others aren't here yet?" he asked.

At that point, three men came out of the alley that led from the street.

"They're just getting here," Skinner said.

Clint looked around. This back area seemed to extend the length of the block, with most of the other buildings along the way being deserted. About a hundred yards away, some targets were set up, and a wooden fence had been erected behind them. Between the targets and the fence, several bales of hay had been set up.

"You want me to shoot at some bull's-eye targets?" Clint asked, using his best "Bellman" tone of disdain.

"You want to shoot at something else?" Sharp asked.

"Well, I had something else in mind, yeah."

As the other three men approached, Sharp made no attempt to introduce them. They simply lined up against the back wall of the saloon and watched.

"What did you have in mind?"

"Why don't you walk down to the other end of the range with Skinner and he'll explain."

Sharp looked from Clint to Skinner and back again, then said to Skinner, "Well, come on."

As Skinner and Sharp walked to the other end of the range, Sharp said, "Are you and Bellman getting to be good friends, Skinner?"

"I took him to Big Milly's like you asked me," Skinner said. "That's all."

"And now you and he have set up some kind of an arrangement to impress me?"

"I just agreed to help out, is all."

"What does he have in mind?"

Skinner reached into his pocket and came out with four red poker chips.

"Poker chips?"

"They're small," Skinner said. "He intends to plug them right in the middle."

"That would be impressive."

As they reached the targets and bales of hay, Skinner said, "He wants you to hold them."

"Me?"

Skinner nodded.

"Is he crazy? How would he like *me* to hold them?"

"Like this," Skinner said.

He splayed his fingers and filled each space with a poker chip, each one facing outward. A man would have to have a large hand to do this, but both Skinner and Sharp qualified.

"He's going to plug each one in the center without knocking them from your hand, so you'll have to close your fingers tightly, like this."

Skinner demonstrated, holding each clip tightly between his fingers.

"He's crazy," Sharp said again. "What if he hits me in the face or something, or shoots off a finger?"

"He won't shoot off a finger," Skinner said. "And as for your face, you can hold your hand over your head, like this."

And so saying, Skinner stuck his hand above his head, the chips facing Clint.

"What's that?" Sandy asked Gentry.

"Must be someone shooting at the firing range."

"This early?"

"They must be testing a new man."

"You mean, like I'll be tested?"

"Maybe."

"Let's go look."

Gentry hesitated a moment, then said, "Okay, this way."

When Skinner raised his hand above his head, Clint was able to see each of the red chips very clearly.

He drew and fired. . . .

Skinner was paralyzed.

He felt the first bullet poke a hole through a chip and barely had time to register what was happening before the second, third and fourth chips were also drilled.

Slowly, he brought his hand down so that both he and Sharp could look at the chips. Each one had a neat round hole right in the center of it.

"You're right," Sharp said to Skinner, "that was impressive."

"Jesus. . . ." Skinner said, and waved his hand as if the chips were hot. They fell to the ground, and Skinner stared at his hand to make sure each finger was still there, and still whole.

Sharp walked away and Skinner followed, his hand vibrating.

When Sandy and Gentry came around the corner, they saw two men walking toward a bearded, long-haired man wearing a buckskin-fringe jacket. One of the men was shaking his hand, as if he'd just been burned.

"The man in front is Sharp," Gentry said.

"The man who runs things."

"Right. The other man is Skinner. He's a pain, a constant complainer. The three men standing against the wall are all instructors and, in this case, judges."

"And the man with the long hair?"

"He's being judged."

"Well," Sharp said, upon reaching Clint, "that *was* very impressive, indeed."

Clint didn't say anything. He ejected the spent shells from his Navy Colt and reloaded. As he holstered it, Skinner caught up to Sharp, and then marched right past him toward Clint.

"You sonofabitch!" he said, swinging.

Clint ducked beneath the blow and allowed Skinner to continue on, off balance. As the man fell to the dirt, Clint turned and saw the man called Gentry standing there, with a blonde woman next to him.

"Damn it, Bellman! You could have killed me! You could have shot off my fingers. You could of—"

Skinner continued his tirade, unaware that Clint was not even listening to him. He was looking past Skinner at the man and woman.

Sandy and Gentry had watched as the long-haired man had sent Skinner sprawling. Skinner began to shout at the man, but he wasn't listening. He was looking at two newcomers.

Sandy examined the man, decided she didn't know, him, then frowned and looked closer.

Or did she?

Now Clint easily recognized the woman, and knew that she was whom he had originally thought she was.

The last time he'd seen her she'd been one of a team of three lady bounty hunters.

What was Sandy Spillane doing here?

TWENTY-THREE

"Get up, Skinner," Sharp said. As Skinner climbed to his feet, Sharp started to speak to Clint, but noticed Gentry and the woman.

"Gentry."

"Yes, sir," Gentry said, moving forward. Sandy hesitated, then followed, lagging slightly behind. She was still throwing an occasional glance at Clint, none of which he missed.

"I didn't expect you back today."

"I didn't expect to get back, but I found someone sooner than I thought."

"The lady?"

"Yep."

Sharp frowned, then looked past Gentry and Sandy Spillane.

"Can you use that gun, miss?"

Sandy, who had been looking at Clint, jerked her eyes away and looked at Sharp.

"When I have to."

"You want to join the League?"

"Why not?"

"Are you prepared to be tested?"

"Sure," she said, shrugging.

"Good," he said. He turned slightly and pointed at Clint. "Kill him."

"What?" she said.

"What?" Clint said.

Sharp looked at Clint and said, "Skinner says he thinks you're a killer. Here's where we find out if the lady is."

"I ain't killing no woman."

"If you don't, then she'll kill you."

Sharp turned to the woman and said, "Won't you?"

Clint's mind was racing. He had no intentions of killing Sandy, or of letting her kill him, but he had to stop this without angering Sharp.

"Sharp, listen—"

"Your test is over, Bellman," Sharp said. "This is the lady's test."

"You mean, if I don't kill him I fail?"

"If you don't kill him, you will probably end up dead," Sharp said. "Think about that."

"Forget it," Clint said.

"What did you say?" Sharp asked.

"I said forget it. I'm not killing a woman, or anyone, just on your say-so."

Sharp looked at Sandy and said, "And you?"

"That depends," she said, "on what I get in return."

"Membership in our League."

"Not enough," she said, shaking her head. "I don't kill for fun, only for profit."

"Skinner," Sharp said.

"Yeah?" Skinner said, still looking at his hand. One. . .two. . .three. . .four. . .five. . .yeah—they were all still there.

"Disarm her."

"What?"

"Take her gun!" Sharp said.

Skinner looked at Sandy Spillane and said, "Just stand fast, lady. All I want is your gun."

"Come and get it."

He walked toward her and suddenly her right fist lashed out, catching him on the butt of the jaw. For the second time in five minutes, Skinner found himself on the ground. Now his jaw stung almost as much as his hand, but he wasn't really hurt, just embarrassed.

He got up and clawed for his gun, but the big blonde produced hers quickly and said, "Don't."

He stopped, staring into the barrel of her gun.

Sharp said, "That's enough. Put the gun away, Miss—"

"Spillane, Sandy Spillane."

"Miss Spillane. Tell me, what have you been doing up to now?"

"I'm a bounty hunter."

"Really?" Sharp said, raising his eyebrows. "That's quite an admission, considering where you are."

"If I was here looking for a price on someone's head —maybe even yours—I sure as hell wouldn't tell you what I am, would I?"

"Perhaps not," Sharp said.

There was an awkward silence, which they all waited for Sharp to break. Sandy looked at Wes Bellman, while Bellman studiously avoided looking her way. She sensed something was wrong. Men usually had trouble taking their eyes *off* her.

"All right," Sharp said.

Sandy and Clint looked at him expectantly, but he didn't say another word. He walked to the back door of the saloon, opened the door, and disappeared.

"What does that mean?" Clint asked.

One of the judges stepped forward and said, "It means you're in."

"Both of us?" Sandy asked.

"Both of you."

The next few moments were given over to introductions. Vaguely, Clint recalled the three men being introduced as Rourke, Johnson and Ransom.

Sandy dutifully shook hands, and then turned to meet the other recent inductee.

"Spillane," she said.

"I know. Wes Bellman."

They shook hands.

"Bellman," she said, mulling the name over. "Have we met before?"

"I don't think so," he said. "I'd remember if we had."

"I guess—" Sandy started, but Gentry put his hand on her hip. A possessive move, Clint thought.

"Come on, Sandy. I'll show you where you bunk."

"All right," Sandy said. "It's nice to meet you, Mr. Bellman. Since we're both new here, maybe we can have a drink together later."

Gentry gave Clint a look that clearly said, "Stay away."

"I'd like that very much," Clint said.

He watched them walk away, and then turned to speak to Skinner, who was the only other person still present.

Skinner's fist exploded on his chin, knocking him backward and to the ground.

"I owed you that!" Skinner said.

Clint looked up, rubbing his chin, and then rested his forearms on his knees.

"Okay," he said, "you owed me."

Skinner reached down to help him to his feet and he accepted the assistance.

"What happened?" Skinner asked. "I thought you were going to shoot them from Sharp's hand."

"Was he going to go for it?"

"No, but—"

"So this worked out even better."

Skinner frowned and said, "You planned it this way all along, didn't you?"

"Well," Clint said, somewhat sheepishly, "maybe. . . ."

"No maybe about it," Skinner said, trying to hang onto his anger. "Between you and that big blonde bitch, I need some time or you and I are going to go at it."

"What about the boardinghouse?" Clint asked as Skinner was walking away.

"Grab your gear and go on over there," Skinner said over his shoulder. "Find an empty room and take it. I'll see you later."

Clint hoped that Skinner would get over his anger. He might need the man if he was going to get a message out to Cartwright.

Thinking about Sandy Spillane and her sudden appearance, he started for the hotel to collect his gear.

TWENTY-FOUR

When the door to the boardinghouse opened, a girl in a peasant blouse, with short hair and small, pert breasts stood there, leaning in the doorway.

"Well," she said.

"You must be Betty."

"That's me. Who are you?"

"Bellman."

"You're new?"

"Right."

"Second one today," Betty said. She looked up and down and said, "At least you're promising."

"Any empty rooms?"

"Plenty. Come on in and I'll show you one."

"Thanks."

As he slipped past her, she came off the door and rubbed against him. It was a nice rub.

She closed the door and said, "Come on upstairs."

"Lead the way."

She did, giving him a pleasant trail to follow. Skinner had indicated that Betty was always in heat, and Clint imagined that he could smell her.

And he reacted.

It occurred to him that a man could easily find himself dead in bed if he stayed a member of the League for too long.

"Where is the other new man staying?" he asked.

"Ha," Betty said, turning to face him at the top of the stairs. She did so quickly, so that he walked into her and had to grab her by the shoulders to keep either one of them from falling.

"The other new person," she said, "is a girl. You like girls?"

He took his hands off her smooth shoulders and said, "I like girls very much."

This one was as cute as a button, but a little too easily had for his tastes.

She led him to a room and opened a door.

"How's this one?" she asked.

"Looks fine."

"Would you like me to stay and help you. . .test it out?"

"Test it out?" he asked, pretending not to understand.

"Yeah, you know, like the bed?"

"Maybe another time, Betty. I've got to unpack, and then I'd like to get a bath."

"Well, let me know if you do. I'm the one who gets the water."

"Oh, well in that case, yeah, I would like a bath."

"Hot or cold?"

"Hot."

"Fifteen minutes, all right?"

"Fine."

"Bath's in the back on the first floor."

"Thanks."

She grinned and said, "When you come down, I'll be ready for you."

As she left, he had a feeling she was talking about herself and not the bath.

He was thinking about Sandy Spillane and Jason Sharp. As much as he hated coincidence, he had to admit that he was apparently the victim here of not one, but two. There was no way either Jason Sharp of Sandy could have know he was coming here. Now that they all *were* here, though, he was going to have to deal with it.

So far, the long hair and beard, along with the false mannerisms, seemed to have worked. Sandy was a bigger threat to his identity because they had seen each other recently, within the past few years. With Sharp, he figured he was fairly safe, because they had not seen each other in over twenty years.

He had to admit that he didn't know Jason Sharp— not this one, anyway. He couldn't predict how the man would react if he found out who Wes Bellman really was, but he was still going to have to make sure that Sandy didn't accidentally give him away, in the event that she recognized him. Also, it might pay to reveal himself to her and find out what she was doing here. She might be able to help.

He dropped his gear on the floor and pulled out a clean shirt, then went downstairs to take his bath.

He wished he could shave off the damned beard. It itched like mad.

TWENTY-FIVE

Len Tobey watched as the man he knew as Tom Sideman walked down the hall to the bathroom in the back of the building. He touched his gun and decided that he'd wait for Sideman to step back out into the hall again. A gunman like him would have the gun close at hand even while in the tub. More than likely, however, when he walked out, his gun would be somewhere other than on his hip, and that would give him the advantage he needed.

This is for you, Jerry. . . .

As he had expected, Betty had more in mind than just drawing his bath, but he had no time for her now—and probably never would. He stopped her cold before she could undress and shooed her out of the room. He was just glad she hadn't *already* stripped. She had a nice, firm little body, and he might not have been able to push her out if she had already been naked.

He dressed and started to leave the room, carrying his shirt, which he had washed in the bathwater before taking his bath. He had his gunbelt slung over his left shoulder, and the shirt in his right hand.

Out in the hall, he saw a man coming his way. For a moment he figured the man was on his way to take a bath, but then he saw the look in the man's eyes.

"I knew it," the man said.

As the man went for his gun, Clint threw his wet shirt and reached for his own gun. The heavy, wet shirt hit the man in the face, and as he groped for it Clint drew his gun and fired. His bullet struck the man in the chest knocking him back. The man drew his gun and discharged it into the ceiling, but it was simply a reflex move—the man was already dead even before his shot struck the ceiling.

Clint started to lean over the dead man when he heard footsteps coming down the hall. He looked up, gun ready, and saw Betty running toward him.

"What happened?"

"This guy tried to kill me."

"Why?"

"I don't know. Maybe I used his bath towel." He removed his wet towel from the man's face and looked at him.

"Do you know him?" the girl asked.

"No," Clint said, staring down at the man who was a stranger to him. "Do you?"

"His name is Tobey, Len Tobey."

Clint frowned. The man's name meant nothing to him, either.

"Do you know Skinner?"

"Sure—"

"Find him and get him over here."

At that moment there were other footsteps coming down the hall and several men burst into view.

"What happened here?"

"This is a new man," Betty said. "Tobey tried to kill him, but the new man got him first."

The three men looked at each other and seemed to accept her explanation.

"I'm going to get Skinner," she said, and pushed past them.

The three men moved down the hall to where Clint was now standing.

"Did you know Tobey?" one of them asked.

"No."

"I guess he knew you, though," another man said.

"Maybe," Clint said. "And maybe he just thought he did."

"You mean he thought you were somebody else?" the third man asked.

"He must have," Clint said, and then realized that that had to be the answer. With his hair and beard, he had resembled someone that Tobey knew, and the man had reacted to that.

It had to be that way, because Clint didn't know the man and there was no way the man could have recognized him.

He made a move to pass the three men in the hall, but they closed it off on him.

"I think maybe we better wait for Skinner," one of them said, and the other two nodded.

Clint decided not to press the issue. After all, he had sent Betty to get Skinner in the first place.

"Okay," he said, "so we'll wait."

When Betty returned with Skinner, the four men were standing apart—Clint on one side of the body, and the other three men on the other. Clint was leaning against the wall with his arms folded.

"What happened?" Skinner asked.

"This jasper drew on me and I killed him."

Clint figured he was better off presenting his case succinctly.

"How did it happen?"

"I was coming out from a bath. He was coming down the hall. He went for his gun—"

"He didn't say anything first?"

"No, nothing. He just went for his gun and I beat him to it."

"Do you know him?"

"No."

"Why would he try to kill you, then?"

Clint pushed away from the wall.

"I don't know, Skinner. All I know is that he tried to kill me and missed. I'm going up to my room."

He walked past the three men, who now let him through after a nod from Skinner.

"Sharp's gonna want to talk to you about this, Bellman," Skinner said.

"You let me know when. I'll be up in my room taking a nap."

As Clint left, one of the men said to Skinner, "He just killed a man and he's gonna take a nap?"

Skinner looked at the man and said, "He's just arrived and already he's one lesson up on you."

TWENTY-SIX

Instead of going up to his room to take a nap, Clint went looking for Sandy Spillane.

He found out that there were only a few women in Lost City who were actually part of the Fast Draw League, and that they lived in a boardinghouse on the other end of town. He went there and knocked on the door. It was answered by a tall, good looking young man and Clint wondered if he served the same purpose here that Betty served at the other boardinghouse.

"I'd like to see Sandy Spillane."

"Is that the new girl?"

"Yes. Is she here?"

"She's upstairs."

"Would you tell her I'm here?"

"What's your name?"

"Wes Bellman."

"She know you?"

"No."

"Why would she want to see you, then?"

Clint studied the man and decided that he probably was the male equivalent of Betty—and not good for much more. A smooth-faced dandy who had been hired to simply care for the needs of the League's women members.

He was pushing his luck.

"Look, friend, just go on up and tell her I'm here. Don't make me come past you and tell her myself."

The man's jaw firmed, but he quickly changed his mind and backed off.

"Wait here."

He went back into the house and then returned several moments later.

"She says you should wait in the living room."

"Show me where it is."

"This way."

Clint entered and followed the young man.

"You don't mind if I don't wait with you?"

"I wouldn't have it any other way. You probably have a lot of work to do."

The man looked as if he wanted to say something, but finally just left the room.

The room—and, in fact, the whole building—was a duplicate of the building he had just come from, but Clint was sure there were many more empty rooms here than there were on the men's side.

"You wanted to see me?" he heard Sandy's voice ask from behind him.

He turned slowly and saw her in the doorway, as strikingly handsome as the last time he had seen her.

"How many people are in the house?"

She shrugged and said, "Teddy is upstairs with Milly Ferris."

"Teddy is the nice boy who let me in?"

She grinned and said, "Yes, he is nice, isn't he?"

"No one else in the house?"

"Not that I know of. Why?" she asked, frowning at him. He could see that she was studying him, as if there was something about him that was bothering her.

Revealing himself to her was the right move, he decided, because in time she would have figured it out for herself, and might possibly have blurted it out.

"Hello, Sandy," he said in his normal tone of voice. He also assumed his normal stance.

"Hello," she said, staring at him. "Am I crazy, or do I know you?"

"We know each other very well, Sandy. We also have two friends in common. How are Anne and Katy, by the way?"

"Anne and Katy," she said, still studying him, frowning mightily now. "They're fine. . . ."

She came into the room and got closer to him, almost close enough to touch, before she reared back, eyes wide and mouth open in surprise.

"It can't be."

"Why not?"

"But you look. . .terrible!"

And with that she was in his arms, pressing herself tightly against him, her mouth eager on his.

"Let's save this for when we're alone," he said a moment later. "Someone might walk in."

"Oh," she said, backing away. "Clint—"

"Bellman," he said, cutting her off, "Wes Bellman."

Shaking her head she asked, "But what are you doing here?"

"I want to ask you the same question," he said. "So I'll go first, and then you, and then maybe we'll see if we can help each other. . . ."

TWENTY-SEVEN

They went out behind the women's boardinghouse instead of staying in the living room, just in case someone walked in on them.

Clint explained that he was there on behalf of the government, who wanted the League's activities stopped before they could turn out more killers.

Sandy then explained that she was there looking for her brother.

"I didn't even know that you had a brother."

She nodded.

"He's ten years younger than I am and somehow got it into his head that he was a gunman. I heard that he got hooked up with the League, and I'm here to get him out."

"Have you seen him since you arrived?"

"No, but I haven't gotten around much."

"The fella who brought you in—"

"Sam Gentry."

"Does he know your brother?"

"I haven't asked him. I'm supposed to be here because he brought me here."

"All right. I'll keep my ears open and see what I can find out. What's your brother's name?"

"Paul."

"Okay. I'll see if he's here."

"Thanks, I appreciate your help. I'm really glad you're here. Now, what can I do to help you. . .and the government, of course?"

"You can leave here."

"What?"

"As soon as possible."

"I don't—"

"Listen to me, Sandy. Someone has to get a message back to Jim West or his boss about where this place is. I don't know how, when or even *if* I'll be able to do it."

"I'm not leaving here without my brother, Clin—"

"Wes."

"Whoever." She pushed away from the wall and faced him angrily.

"I came here to get my brother out and I'm not leaving until I do."

"I'll find him and get him out, Sandy—"

"That would be your second priority. . .Wes. . .and finding him is *my* first."

"Sandy—"

"How about I stay and take care of your little problem, and *you* leave?"

"Sandy—"

"You're repeating yourself."

Clint stared at her and realized that he was facing an immovable object.

"All right," he said, "but we've got to stay together on this. If this thing blows up in either one of our faces, we'll have to fight our way out."

"We've fought together before. Now, what about some other things that we've done before?"

"What about Sam Gentry? My guess is you had to get pretty friendly with him and get him to bring you here."

"A little."

"And I'd also guess that he's acting more than a bit possessive."

"So?"

"So we don't need extra added trouble. You keep playing up to him; see if you can locate your brother."

"And what do you need?"

"Some idea of exactly where this town is located. When I get a message out I've got to be able to tell them exactly where to find this place."

"All right. . .but afterward—"

"Right," he said, touching her arm, "afterward. You go back inside and I'll circle around. I don't think we should be seen together alone."

"All right," she said, opening the back door.

As he started to walk away she called out to him.

"Wes?"

"Yes?" he said, turning around.

"Consider yourself kissed goodbye—for now."

He threw her a kiss and continued on.

He was halfway back to his own boardinghouse when someone called his name. He turned and found Skinner approaching him.

"I've been looking for you."

"Is that a fact?"

"I thought you said you were going to be taking a nap in your room."

"I decided to go for a walk. Do I have to ask for permission to go for a walk?"

"Sharp wants to see you."

"About what?"

"Jesus Christ, man, what do you think? You killed one of his men!"

"I'm one of his men."

"That remains to be seen," Skinner said. "Come on, let's go."

TWENTY-EIGHT

Skinner took Clint to Sharp's office in the saloon, where Sharp was waiting behind his desk.

"That's all, Skinner," Sharp said. "You can go."

"But—"

"You can go, Skinner."

Skinner hesitated, then left.

Clint sat and waited for Sharp to initiate the conversation.

"Does the name Tom Sideman mean anything to you?"

"Sideman. . ." Clint repeated, mulling it over. It sounded familiar and he said so.

"Why?" he asked.

"The man you killed was Len Tobey."

"I know that."

"His friend, Bill Evans, was with him when you rode in with Skinner."

"And?"

"Tobey said that he thought you were a man named Tom Sideman, and that you had killed his brother five years ago. What do you say to that?"

"What do you want me to say? My name is Wes Bellman. I never saw this fella Tobey before he tried to kill me today. I defended myself."

"So I understand."

"Sideman," Clint said again. Now he remembered. "Wasn't he a two-bit gunman, a few years back?"

"That's what my information says," Sharp said, picking up a yellow slip of paper from his desk. "Sideman was killed three years ago in Laredo."

"Then if he's dead, how could I be him?"

"You can't."

"Then Tobey was mistaken."

"So it appears."

"So what was this all about?"

"I just wanted to see how you would react."

"And did I pass?"

"You did."

"Can I go now?"

"No, you can't."

"More testing?"

"Would you like a drink?"

"Sure."

Sharp stood up and poured two whiskeys from a small bar that was set up near his desk. He handed one to Clint, took his own and sat down again behind the desk.

"I need a good man."

"For what?"

"I need someone I can depend on to be my. . .right hand, for want of a better phrase."

"What about Skinner?"

"Skinner?" Sharp said, laughing. "Skinner's one of my problems."

"Why is that?"

"He wants to take over, Wes. Don't tell me he hasn't tried to recruit you."

"As a matter of fact, he has implied something to that effect."

"You see? And I'm sure he's recruited others. I've got to try and keep this thing together, Wes, and I think you can help me do that."

"How?"

"You're good with a gun. That's already been established, and the word has spread. Skinner is hoping to use you to get by me."

"Does he need my help for that? I understood he was pretty fast."

"He's fair. I've got someone who's faster, but I'd still like to have you on my side."

"What's in it for me?"

"Money."

"No beating around the bush, huh?"

"Money," Sharp said, "and a lot of it."

"How much?"

"We can talk about that later. Believe me, it's more than you've ever had before."

"And all I've got to do is kill Skinner?"

"If it comes to that, I've got it covered. I need you to stand beside me if some of Skinner's followers react. . . badly to his death."

"I see."

"Take today to consider it," Sharp said, raising his glass. "This is good whiskey, isn't it?"

"Yes, it is."

"Money buys good whiskey."

"Money buys a lot of things," Clint said. He drank his whiskey down and put the glass on Sharp's desk. "I don't need the day to think it over. I'm in."

"Well, fine," Sharp said. "Have another drink and then we'll discuss exactly what I want you to do. . . ."

What Sharp wanted was very simple. He wanted Clint

to circulate among the men, get to know them, and see just who was on Skinner's side and who was on Sharp's.

"In other words, who's loyal to the League and who isn't," Clint said.

"Right."

"I should be able to do that."

"If you don't mind, I'll try to recruit that new woman right away, before Skinner can get to her."

"I don't have any objections."

"Good."

On his way out, Clint brought up one other thing.

"This other man, Bill Evans. Just how friendly was he with Len Tobey?"

"You mean is he going to come after you?"

"That's what I mean."

"If he does," Sharp said, "kill him, too."

When Clint left, he found Johnny Skinner waiting for him outside.

"Get bawled out?"

"Royally."

"I don't know why. It was clear that it was self-defense."

"Did you know about this 'Sideman' business?" Clint asked.

"I talked to Bill Evans, yeah."

"And you knew that Sharp had checked it out?"

"Sure."

"And found out that Sideman was dead?"

"Yes."

"It might have helped if I had known that going in."

"Yeah," Skinner said, "I guess it might have."

"Pay-back, huh?"

"Where are you going now?"

"I'm going to take that nap I wanted before. What about you?"

"What about me?"

"Still mad about before, or was this pay-back enough for you?"

"No," Skinner said. "I still don't like it, but I'm not mad."

"Good. We'll talk later, then."

"Sure," Skinner said, "we'll talk. . . ."

TWENTY-NINE

Over the course of the next few days, Clint met as many of the League members—instructors and students —as he could, and became friendly with a few of them.

The ones who he made a point of befriending were the instructors. He drank with them, played poker with them, and went to Big Milly's with them.

With the students, he simply made a point of cultivating them, not treating them the way most of the other instructors did.

He also managed to ascertain that there were at least three instructors—Bill Evans among them—who were likely to side with Skinner when he made his move against Sharp.

Which meant that they might eventually be of some use to him, as well.

The day after he had spoken with Sharp and taken him up on his offer, he had gone to see Sandy.

In the living room of her boardinghouse, she said, "I thought we weren't supposed to be seen together?"

"That's changed," he said, and told her why.

"That means he trusts you."

"Not necessarily," Clint said. "It means he wants to use me."

"And you're going to let him."

"For a while. Meanwhile, let's just make like I'm recruiting you."

"Oooh," Sandy said, moving closer, "and what method do you intend to use?"

"Whatever method comes naturally," he said taking her into his arms.

Now, three days later, he was starting to wonder if he was ever going to get a message out. Of course, he was in no immediate danger—Sharp had given no sign of recognizing him—but he was still anxious to get this over with, if only to finally be able to shave off the goddamned beard.

Clint was conducting a class of five in sharp shooting —a waste of time and effort—when Sam Gentry came over and began to watch.

"No, no," Clint was saying to one of the students, "don't jerk the trigger like that—"

"Why don't you show them, instead of telling them," Gentry called out.

Clint turned and looked at Gentry. The man had been sending looks his way from the first day he had arrived with Sandy—and lately even moreso, because Clint and Sandy had been seen together quite a bit.

"Don't you have something to do?" Clint asked.

"Not really. Come on, Bellman—show these fellas what you can do, huh?"

Clint turned and looked at his students. They were not students in the true sense of the word—that is, school-aged kids. They were grown men who were deemed to have abilities with a gun that could possibly be refined.

Now one of the oldest said, "Yeah, Bellman—show us."

"That's all for today," Clint told the five men, who exchanged glances and then accepted the early dismissal.

When they were gone, Clint approached Gentry, stopping within arm's length.

"Look, Gentry, I don't appreciate this intrusion, so why don't we agree that it won't happen again, huh?"

"Why don't we agree that you'll stay away from Sandy Spillane?"

"Well, now, that would be up to the lady, wouldn't it?"

"No, it's up to me." Gentry prodded Clint in the chest with his forefinger and said, "Just take my advice and stay away from her."

"Take my advice and stay away from me," Clint said. With that he slapped Gentry across the face open-handed, knowing that it would enrage him.

Gentry's eyes flared and he went for his gun, but before he could reach it Clint plucked it out of his holster.

"Give it back!" Gentry shouted.

Clint slid the gun into his belt and Gentry swung at him. He easily avoided the blow and stiff-armed Gentry in the chest, knocking him to the ground.

The man glared up at Clint, who knew he was angry because he had been disarmed and knocked down and Clint had not even used a closed fist.

"You can get your gun back from Sharp, Gentry. I'm sure he'll be interested in how you lost it."

"Bastard!"

"My advice to you now is don't bother getting up until I'm gone. It wouldn't be healthy."

Clint walked away, leaving the enraged man on the ground, shouting obscenities at him.

"Do you think that was wise?" Sharp asked as Clint laid Gentry's gun on his desk.

"Maybe not, but it gave me an excuse to see you without anyone getting suspicious."

"Why did you want to see me?"

"Well, I'm pretty sure that Skinner has Evans and a couple of other instructors on his side already, and he's working on a few of the others, as well."

"And what about the students?"

"Haven't gotten close enough to any of them yet to tell, but I'm working on it."

"And the new woman? What's her name?"

"Spillane, Sandy Spillane. She's ready to go along with me."

"I wonder how you managed that?"

"Just some gentle persuasion, and a few promises."

"What about Gentry?"

"Well, because of the woman, I think Gentry is pretty much riding the fence. He doesn't like Skinner—"

"—and he hates you."

"Right."

"I suppose I'll have to talk to Gentry myself."

"Make him think he's real important to you. That's why I took his gun. So he'll have to come in and see you."

"All right. Do you have any idea when Skinner is planning to try a takeover?"

"Not yet. As soon as I do, I'll let you know."

"Very well."

Clint started for the door, then turned back.

"Am I an accepted member of this outfit, yet?"

"Accepted? Yes, I guess you are. . .to a certain extent. Why?"

"I was thinking about taking a buggy outside of town—"

"With a young woman?"

"If that's permitted."

"You can do anything you want with any of the women in town," Sharp said, "but that's the operative phrase—*in town.*"

"You mean I can't leave?"

"Bellman, I mean no one leaves town, not without my okay, and I only give that for my own reasons. So, pick out your lady and do what you like, but *don't* leave town."

Leaving the office, Clint wondered how the hell he was supposed to get a message out if he couldn't leave town.

He had not yet broached the subject with anyone, but the piece of paper on Sharp's desk clinched it for him. He knew there wasn't a telegraph office in town, but he figured that a "sharp" operator like Jason Sharp wouldn't want to be out of touch with the rest of the world.

He was going to have to find Sharp's personal telegraph line.

THIRTY

That evening Clint discussed Sharp's telegraph line with Sandy while they sat in the Lost City Saloon.

"I haven't seen any wires, Wes," she said. She'd gotten pretty good at calling him by his new name.

"They could be strung a distance out of town, and then buried underground at the point where they enter the town. That could be why he doesn't want anyone wandering from town."

"Then what we've got to do is find that telegraph line and use it to send out your message."

"He's got to have an operator, and I'd guess one other man who knows about it. That makes three."

"One of the men has to be Philip, his. . .I don't know what he is."

"Is that the black manservant he has?" Clint asked. "I've heard some talk about him."

"I've heard Gentry talk about him, and it sounds to me like he's more than just a manservant, or a butler. Apparently, they're very close."

"Then we probably wouldn't get it from him. There's got to be an operator, Sandy. We've got two choices: We can try to find the operator, or try to find the wire and trace it back to town."

"That means leaving town, which is risky."

"I'll have to do it after dark."

"Let me do it. You're more visible than I am."

He gave her an exaggerated look and said, "You've got to be kidding."

"I mean Sharp might even be having you watched. He's going to want to be very sure about you if you're going to be his number one man."

"Number two, if what you say about Philip is right. You know, I'd be real curious to find out Philip's last name."

"Why?"

Clint shrugged.

"Just curious."

"You haven't been in Sharp's house yet, have you?"

"No."

"From what I hear, Philip rarely leaves the house, so to get a look at him you'd have to get inside."

"First things first. I want to try and find that wire tonight."

"How will you do that?"

"Well," Clint said, "I think we could start by you inviting me to your room."

Later that night, Clint accompanied Sandy Spillane into her boardinghouse and up to her room. Through the right wall of her room they were able to hear some activity that undoubtedly involved a man and a woman.

"That's got to be Teddy entertaining Kitty."

"Kitty?"

"Kitty Crawford. She gets the most use out of him, I hear. She ain't exactly a spring chicken, but she's supposed to be a fair hand with a gun."

Clint walked to the window and looked out at the

back of the house. The room was on the second floor, making it a pretty good drop, but he figured his knees could take it.

"What are you planning to do?"

"Drop down out of this window when the rest of the town is asleep and go looking for that telegraph line. Then I'm going to try and trace it back."

"But if it's underground like you say, how are you going to trace it without digging it up? And digging it up is going to give away the fact that *somebody* was looking for it."

"I'm willing to bet that it runs in a straight line to whatever building houses the telegraph key. I'm also willing to bet that the telegraph isn't far from Sharp's house—if it's not in Sharp's house itself."

"What about a horse?"

"That's a problem. I'd prefer to do this on foot, but the fact that we can't see the telegraph line means that it's too far for me to look for it on foot."

"Either that or it doesn't exist."

"Oh, it exists, all right," Clint said. "That's something else I'm betting on."

"What happens if you get caught?"

"I'll have to think up some kind of story and hope it holds up."

"When are you going to do it?"

Clint looked up at the night sky.

"The saloon here closes at twelve. I'll wait until about one. Everyone should be either asleep or otherwise occupied by then."

"Well then, that's what we should do until it's time for you to go."

"Sleep?" he asked, turning.

"No," she said, dropping her shirt to the floor, "become otherwise occupied.''

This was the first time since her arrival in town that they had gone to bed together.

He remembered her body. Large, firm breasts, slightly convex belly, heavy thighs, and that sweet, sweet place between her legs, just behind the pale forest of hair.

Her nipples were large and as he nibbled on them they became larger. She ran her hands over his back as he continued to explore her big breasts with his mouth and tongue, and then he worked his way down over her belly. The hair between her legs was fine and fragrant, and he poked through it with his tongue until he could taste her. She started as his tongue entered her, then she relaxed and gave herself up to the sensations as he swirled his tongue around, darting, tasting. . .he slid his hands beneath her, cupping her big, firm buttocks, squeezing her as he found her clit and sucked on it.

"Oh, Jesus, Clint," she said, using his real name in the heat of the moment, but he didn't mind. . .not then.

He lapped at her avidly, alternately circling her clit with his tongue, and gently sucking on it. Finally, as her belly began to tremble, he did away with gentleness. He pursued his lips, sucked her clit in and lashed it with his tongue until she moaned and lifted her hips off the bed. It was all he could do to maintain contact with her as she thrashed about on the bed, but he did so until she clawed at him, trying to draw him up to her.

He moved atop her and she reached for his swollen penis with both hands, guiding it to the proper entry point . . . and in.

"Yes, yes, oh God, yes!" she moaned over and over

again as he slammed into her.

She was a big girl and he had no fear of hurting her. The room was filled with the sound of his flesh slapping hers as they came together again and again, with Sandy applying as much pressure as he was.

"Jesus," he said, gritting his teeth, because the time was coming and he didn't want it to end yet.

He fought it for as long as he could, but finally she drew it out of him—dragged it out of him in long, hard, almost painful spurts that seemed as if they'd never end.

"My God," she said later, "I thought you'd never stop filling me up."

"So did I."

"Anne is going to kill me, you know."

"Why should she?"

"Because she loves you."

Clint thought about Anne Archer—red hair, sultry, with full, pouty lips and dark eyebrows. A slender body, much smaller than Sandy's, but no less firm. He had to admit that of the three of them—Anne, Sandy and Katy Little Flower—the red-haired young woman was his favorite.

But love. . . ?"

"She won't know unless you tell her."

"Oh, I'll tell her," Sandy said. "We're almost like sisters, Clint. I wouldn't dare not tell her. Besides, she'd know, anyway."

"What are you doing?" he asked as her hand snaked down beneath the sheet.

"Well, if she's going to kill me, I figure I might as well go all the way. . . ."

She slid the sheet away from them and used her hand on him until he was standing straight and tall again.

"I want to suck you. . . ."

She slid down so that she was nose to head with his stiff cock and stuck her tongue out to lick it, up and down, slowly, sensuously, while holding it at the base with one hand and fondling his balls with the other.

"Jesus, Sandy," he said as she opened her mouth and lowered it over him, taking an amazing amount of his length inside, "*you're* going to kill *me*. . . ."

THIRTY-ONE

On his third try at climbing out of Sandy's bed, he made it. This time she didn't claw for him and drag him back to her hot embrace and give him good reason to stay.

Maybe *he'd* finally worn *her* out.

Sure.

"Time to go," she said, watching him dress.

It wasn't a question, but he said, "Yes."

"I've been meaning to ask you."

"What?"

"Where's that fancy gun you always used to wear?"

"I didn't feel it was wise to wear it. It might have given me away."

"Like Duke. You left him behind, too?"

"Yeah."

"Well, I guess you can shoot with anything, can't you?"

"Just about."

He strapped on the Navy Colt and was ready to go.

"Be careful, Clint—I mean, Wes."

"I'll be back to help you find your brother, Sandy."

"That's not what I meant."

"I know. . .but I just wanted you to know that I didn't forget."

He went to the window, opened it, dangled first one leg and then the other, and dropped down.

Clint made his way to the livery stable without being seen and found it unlocked. Supposedly, there was no reason for any doors in Lost City to be locked. He doubted the wisdom of such a decision, but was glad it existed here and now.

He saddled his horse and walked him out of the livery and, using a side street, out of the town. When he felt he was far enough out, he mounted up and started his search for the telegraph lines.

Clint circled the town until he felt he was behind, or at least near, Sharp's house, then began working his way away from the town in a zig-zag pattern—and he found what he was looking for.

The lines were not at all far from town, but they had been strung through dense trees rather than bare poles, and thus were hidden from sight. No doubt if he were to ride a few more miles from town the lines would start to show up on bare poles, but near town the trees were more than adequate cover for the secret telegraph lines.

He followed the lines with difficulty, but the bright moonlight kept it from being impossible. He finally found the last tree in line. Dismounting, he found that the line ran down the side of it and into the ground.

Mounting his horse, he started traveling in a straight line, hoping that the line didn't veer away at some point. It would make sense for them to work it in a straight line, because that would have been the easiest way to do it.

His decision was vindicated when he realized that some excavating had been done—trees and bushes uprooted—to allow for the wire to continue to run straight.

He had been right after all.

When he was fairly close to town he dismounted, tied off his horse, and went the rest of the way on foot. Soon he was able to hear laughing and music. He saw the building that the noise was coming from and knew it had to be the right one.

Moving as quietly as possible, he approached the rear of the building and began to study it. After about ten minutes he found what he was looking for, low down to the ground. The wire appeared, and then quickly disappeared into the wall.

This was it—the building where the telegraph key was. And he'd managed to find it before half the night has passed.

He hurried back to his horse and then walked him toward the livery stable, hoping that he would continue to go unnoticed. Luck was with him and he unsaddled the animal, hastily rubbed him down and left him some feed.

Making his way back to the women's boardinghouse, he found himself standing beneath Sandy's window and slapped his forehead.

In his haste, he had not made plans for getting back *into* her room.

Smart, he told himself sarcastically, very smart.

Suddenly, a length of sheet fell to the ground and he could see that several sheets had been knotted together. Hurriedly, and as quietly as possible, he used the sheets to scale the wall and reach Sandy's window. She was there to grab his arm and help him in.

"Quick," she said, "pull the sheets back in."

As he did so he said, "What makes you so smart?"

"I figured I had you so distracted with my body that you were sure to forget something."

"And you were right," he said, closing the window.

"And now you owe me."

"I sure do."

"How do you think I should collect?"

Suddenly her nightgown fell away, leaving her naked and pale in the moonlight, and he said, "I'll bet we can think of something."

"Did you find it?" she asked later.

"I found it."

"Where is it?"

"It's somewhere in the busiest building in town," he answered. "Big Milly's whorehouse."

"Well," Sandy said, "won't you have fun finding it."

THIRTY-TWO

Clint decided that his best bet was to try to find the telegraph key at night, so he spent the rest of *that* night with Sandy, and would then go to Big Milly's the *next* night.

In the morning, Sandy woke him in a pleasant way that quickly turned urgent. He picked his hips up off the bed in response to the pressure of her sucking mouth and then moaned aloud as he erupted into her mouth.

"What a way to wake up, huh?" she asked, looking up at him from between his legs and wiggling her eyebrows.

"A man could have a heart attack like that."

He rolled out from beneath her and stood up.

"Where are you going?"

"I'm going back to my boardinghouse to have a bath."

"And who draws your bath for you? Little Betty?"

"What do you know about Little Betty?"

"She was pointed out to me. Pretty little thing, isn't she?"

"I hadn't noticed."

"I've heard she can go all night. Now a man could have a heart attack with her very easily."

"I'd rather have it with you," he said, pulling on his

167

boots. "Besides, what about Little Teddy."

She wrinkled her nose and said, "Not my type."

"You don't like lean, smooth-faced, good-looking men, huh?"

"I don't like boys," she said, reaching for him. He ducked away and strapped his gun.

"Let's have dinner tonight, before I go to Big Milly's," he said. "You can give me some pointers."

"Believe me, you don't need any pointers."

"I'll take that as a compliment," he said on his way to the door.

"It was meant as one," she called after him.

As he stepped out into the hall, the door of the next room opened and Teddy appeared bare-chested and looking exhausted. Whoever Kitty was, she must have had a lot of energy to be able to wear out a young stud like he was supposed to be, Clint thought.

"A man could have a heart attack like that," Clint told the younger man, and then started downstairs.

Sam Gentry was not only incensed at the treatment he had received at the hands of Wes Bellman—including the embarrassment of having to retrieve his gun from Sharp's office—he was also livid over the obvious fact that Bellman had just spent the night with Sandy Spillane—his woman! The woman he had found and brought to the League!

Gentry was waiting outside the women's boarding-house for Wes Bellman to come out. He'd seen Bellman in action with a gun and did not think he could take him fair and square, but that wasn't an issue here. He intended to take care of Bellman and explain it away later.

All he wanted right now was to put a bullet in Bellman where it would do the most good—or harm.

• • •

Johnny Skinner was dragging his ass to breakfast when he saw Wes Bellman step out of the women's boardinghouse. He was thinking about the ham and eggs served at the small cafe on this end of town. He stopped when he saw Bellman and wondered which of the League's women he'd been visiting? Kitty? No, she'd be too busy wearing out that pretty boy, Teddy. What about the dark-haired Latin who was the ex-wife of the Mexican bandido? Wait a minute. That new blonde who came to town with Gentry. . . .

Skinner saw Gentry just then, coming from the alley next to the boardinghouse—and he had his gun out. There was no mistaking what he meant to do with it.

Skinner drew his gun quickly and fired.

Clint was crossing the street when he heard the two shots, one right on the heels of the other. He turned quickly and saw Sam Gentry fall to the ground, his gun having discharged into the ground.

He walked over to the fallen man to check him over and found that he was dead as a result of one well-placed shot in the heart. Johnny Skinner came walking up at that point, still holding his gun.

"That was careless," Skinner said.

"I guess I owe you."

Skinner shrugged.

"I saw him laying for you, and I've got some time invested in you. When I make my move on Sharp, I hope you'll remember this."

"I guess I won't have much choice."

"I'll go and let Sharp know what happened here."

At that point Sandy came running out, hair tousled and gun in hand.

"What happened?"

Clint indicated the fallen form of Sam Gentry.

"He tried to shoot me in the back."

"Did you kill him?"

"No," he admitted. "I didn't even see him. Johnny Skinner killed him."

She looked down at Gentry and said, "Jesus, this is my fault."

"It's nobody's fault but Gentry's, Sandy. Just keep in mind that you're here to find your brother. Go on back inside. This is all finished."

As she went back inside, he thought that this was just what he needed, to be beholden to Johnny Skinner when he was looking to put this whole operation away.

THIRTY-THREE

Clint was a bit surprised that over the course of the day he hadn't heard from Jason Sharp about Sam Gentry's death. Then again, if Skinner had done as he said and gone to Sharp's office, then the whole story had already been put before the Fast Draw League's leader.

Since there was nothing he could do about the telegraph key until that evening, he spent a good portion of the day looking for Sandy Spillane's brother. However, he had to do so without asking any specific questions about young Paul Spillane, so as not to arouse any suspicion.

As darkness began to fall, he met Sandy at the same cafe for which Johnny Skinner had been headed that morning.

Sandy was waiting at a table, looking glum and depressed. Clint didn't blame her. He was pretty glum himself, anxious to get this over with and get back to his life. He promised himself that, friend or no friend, Jim West was not going to draft him into any more missions for the United States Secret Service.

"Have you ordered?" he asked, taking a seat across from her.

"Not yet."

"Why so glum?"

"Let's order, and then talk about it."

They ordered simply—steak, potatoes and biscuits, and a pot of coffee. As an afterthought, they each ordered a mug of cold beer.

"Well?" he asked.

"I spent the whole day looking for Paul in this town, Clint. He's just not here."

"Well, I also spent my day doing the same thing and I've come to the same conclusion. Maybe your information was just wrong, Sandy. . . . And if it was, that's good news."

"Well," she said grudgingly, "I guess if he's not here, I should stop worrying about him. After all, he's grown up now."

"Yes, he is."

"He'd probably keep in touch with me if he knew where I was. I guess we both travel around a lot."

"You certainly do, you and your partners."

"I know."

"It's no life for a woman."

Sandy eyes flared and she said, "Don't start that."

"I'm sorry," he said, raising his hands in a defensive gesture.

"I don't like anyone telling me what my life should be like just because I'm a woman."

At that point the waitress came with their dinners, set them down in front of them, and said, "Good for you, honey. You tell him."

As she left they looked at each other and then laughed, any tension that might have existed now broken.

"You'd better eat up," she said to him, "you have a busy night ahead of you."

"I don't think we're both thinking the same way about this."

"Well, you'll have to take some poor girl up to her room and just wear her out before you can leave her, won't you?" Her eyes were wide in feigned innocence. "I mean, how else can you work it?"

"I don't know," Clint said, "but after last night I don't think I could wear anyone out."

"You wore me out."

"That's what I mean. That was last night. I need some more time to recuperate."

"Believe me," she said, grinning, "if you get the right girl you won't have any trouble rising to the occasion."

"Hey," she said laughing, "that's a joke, you know."

"Eat your dinner."

After dinner they ordered another pot of coffee, which Clint drank virtually on his own, and then they left the cafe together.

"I've got an idea," Clint said.

"So do I," she said, linking his arm with hers.

"No, not that idea—not tonight, anyway."

"Then what?"

"Why don't you saddle your horse tonight and ride out of here? I mean, it's pretty obvious that Paul isn't here, so you've got no reason to stay any longer."

"Sure I do."

"What?"

"You might need my help."

"I'll be fine, Sandy—"

"You're in this town all alone and it's full of killers, or would-be killers," she added sarcastically. "Of course you're fine."

"No, I mean it. I'll find that telegraph key, send my message and get out myself."

"Tonight?"

"Tonight."

"Well, good," she said. "Then we can leave together."

"Why don't you leave ahead of me, and I'll catch up with you."

"No chance."

He started to speak again but she cut him off.

"Besides, what kind of message are you going to send? We still don't know where this place is."

"I've been thinking about that. I think I can narrow it down enough to give the Secret Service some time to get a force mobilized, and then when I reach the next town I can send a second message with the exact location."

"So, why don't we just leave now?"

He stopped and said, "You leave now, Sandy. I want to get to that telegraph key—"

"And I'll be waiting out here for you when you come out. I'll saddle both our horses and then we can leave. I don't have anything in my room that I can't leave behind."

He thought a moment, then nodded shortly.

"All right—I don't have anything I can't leave behind, either. Get the horses saddled and I'll meet you at the livery stable."

"Good. Be careful now."

"I will."

"Don't let any of those young girls in there cripple you."

THIRTY-FOUR

Something was wrong. It had been too easy.

Clint was about to enter the room where he could hear the chattering of a telegraph key, and he was thinking *this was just too easy.*

Clint had entered Big Milly's and, given the opportunity to look her stable over, picked out the most weary looking whore he could find. She was a fortyish brunette with some grey in her hair, and a body that was beginning to sag. When he chose her, she rose to her feet resolutely and, shoulders sagging, led him up the stairs to her room.

Once inside she removed her robe, revealing to him large, pendulous, brown tipped breasts and too thin thighs. Around her waist was a small roll of fat that would probably increase monthly, until she'd be in no shape to function as a whore.

"Well, how do you want it?" she asked.

"How about not at all?"

"What?"

"You look like you could use a donation to your retirement fund."

"I don't understand."

"How about a hundred?"

"Hey, it's only twenty—"

"So give Big Milly twenty dollars and you keep the other eighty."

As confused as she was, that appealed to her.

"And what do I have to do for it?"

"Nothing."

"Nothing?"

"Just. . .go to bed and take a nap."

She regarded him quizzically, scratched her belly and said, "Let's see the money."

He took out the hundred dollars and handed it to her.

"And what are you going to be doing?"

"That's none of your business."

"Well, mister," she said, getting into bed, "even if you're gonna rob this place, I wish you luck."

"How often is the hall outside traveled?"

"Only when we're bringing a customer up or down."

"There's a room in this building nobody ever goes in —"

"How did you know that?"

"Lucky guess. Where is it?"

"In the back of the building. There's another hall at the end of this one, and the room is at the end of it."

"Okay. What's your name?"

"Helen."

"Helen, take the money and take your nap and don't come out of this room for at least an hour."

"Mister, my naps take a lot longer than that."

Clint opened the door of her room, checked the hall and then slipped out. He made his way to the end, turned right, and that's when he heard the chattering.

And that's when he started thinking that it had been too easy.

The chattering was the bait to draw him into the

room, and suddenly he wasn't so anxious to go in.

He started to back away from the door when he heard the unmistakable sound of a hammer being cocked behind him.

"I thought you wanted to get inside?"

He recognized the voice: Johnny Skinner.

"Surprised?"

"Yes."

"Let's go inside."

"Sharp waiting in there?"

"Yes."

"I thought you and he were—"

"We cut a new deal, one that includes you out."

"Why?"

"Because Sharp promised me something new."

"Like what?"

"Like a chance at a living legend—the Gunsmith." Skinner came forward and, gesturing with his gun, said, "That's you, pal."

THIRTY-FIVE

Inside the room, Sharp was sitting at a desk while Philip sat at the telegraph key, working it. He wasn't sending any message, he was just making some noise with it.

"All right. Philip," Sharp said, "the fish has taken the bait. You can stop."

The black man stopped and turned in his seat. Clint noticed that he was wearing a gun, and wondered if that was normal.

"Hello, Clint."

"Jason. You've come a long way."

"So have you. The Gunsmith. You've got quite a reputation."

"It's exaggerated."

Sharp laughed.

"I don't think so. Even twenty years ago you were handy with a gun."

"And you were quite different twenty years ago."

"People change."

"I've noticed that."

"I listened and learned, Clint. I turned my whole life around—"

"And founded the Fast Draw League."

"Right."

"What do you know about guns, Jason?"

"Nothing. I keep people around me who do."

"Like me," Skinner said. He'd holstered his gun by now, having tucked Clint's Navy Colt into his belt.

"Not really, Skinner," Jason Sharp said, and looked at Philip.

"What's going on?"

"Philip is going to take care of you for me, Skinner. I can't afford to have someone as ambitious as you around."

"Him? The nigger? What's he gonna do?"

"He's going to put you in your grave, Skinner," Clint said, studying the black man. It was the first time he'd seen him since he'd been there, and he recognized him.

"Don't you know who he is?" Clint asked the confused Skinner.

"He's a nigger houseboy."

"He's Seth Philips. A lot of years back he called himself the Midnight Gun."

"I thought that was just a. . .a legend," Skinner said, staring wide-eyed at the black man.

"Well, there he is," Clint said, "a living legend. You wanted one, and now you've got one."

"He's right, Skinner," Jason Sharp said. "See what you can do."

"Now wait a minute—"

"Philips is going for his gun, Skinner. I'd advise you to go for yours."

Skinner eyed the black man, Seth Philips, whose face was like stone.

Suddenly, the black man's hand flashed for his gun and Clint could barely believe the speed with which he moved. Skinner didn't even have a chance to clear leather when a bullet from Philips' gun slammed him in the chest. As he fell, he slumped between Clint and the other two men and Clint made his move.

As Skinner moved across him, Clint reached for his Navy Colt in the dead man's belt, grabbed it and gave the falling body a push. Sharp, who had been rising, was hit by Skinner and driven back into his chair and over backward. He struggled to get out from beneath the man's dead weight.

Clint and Philips faced each other, both with gun in hand.

"What's it going to be, Seth?"

The black man smiled, revealing teeth gone yellow, and holstered his gun.

For a moment, Clint considered shooting the man where he stood. It would have been the smart thing to do—but then he'd never claimed to be smart.

He holstered his gun, as well.

Sharp finally struggled free of Skinner in time to watch.

Seth Philips' hand flashed for his gun, a triumphant look on his face. He didn't watch the Gunsmith's hand, he watched the man's eyes. Therefore, he didn't see Clint's hand move, or he would have known that he was about to be a dead man.

Philips was just bringing his gun up when Clint fired. The bullet struck the black man in the chest and his smile turned to a grimace. The look was more a one of disgust with himself than one of pain—but he died, nevertheless.

Clint immediately turned his gun toward Sharp, who, having extricated himself from beneath Skinner, raised his hands while still seated on the floor.

"I'm unarmed!"

"That's a shame," Clint said. "Get up."

It would have been easier to kill him, because with any living being, if you cut off the head the body died, and that would have been the way to put an end to the Fast Draw League. Now he and Sandy were going to have to take Sharp with them.

"Let's go."

"Where?"

"We're going to take a moonlight ride—and if you say one wrong word to anyone, your riding days will be over. Do you understand?"

"I understand."

Clint holstered his gun and they walked out of the room, out of the building, and over to the livery without being approached.

"What happened?" Sandy asked.

"I had a little trouble, and as a result we have a passenger." He turned to Sharp and said, "Pick out a horse and saddle him up."

Sharp saddled a big bay and mounted and they left town that way, with Clint in the lead and Sandy bringing up the rear. Sharp refused to tell them what the nearest town was, but Clint knew they'd find it without his help. He rode due west, figuring the worst thing they could do was hit Texas.

They didn't have to go quite that far.

By morning they reached a town called Little Falls, which had both of the things they needed—a telegraph operator, and a lawman with a jail.

The Sheriff was just pushing Sharp into a cell when Clint asked the question he'd been wanting to ask since the night before.

"When did you know it was me, Jason? I mean, it has been a long time and I almost didn't recognize you."

Sharp looked at Clint through the bars, and at one point Clint thought the man wasn't going to answer him, but finally he did.

"You had me fooled until you did that demonstration," Sharp said. "Nobody could shoot like that but you and Hickok, and Hickok is dead. After that I took a good, long hard look at you, Clint, and even under that hair I saw that it was you. You missed a big opportunity last night."

"What was that?"

"I was going to offer you half of everything."

"Well, now you've got nothing, Jason, and half of nothing is nothing. If you don't mind, I'll leave you now. I'm in bad need of a shave."

THIRTY-SIX

"Mmm," Sandy said, "that was luscious."

She was looking down between her legs at Clint's face, which was much more recognizable now. The long hair and beard were gone, and his jaw was slightly pink from the shave.

"It was more than that," he said, "it was downright delicious."

"Let me see," she said, reaching for him.

She drew him up so that she could kiss him, open-mouthed, her tongue darting about, seeking his.

"You know, you're right," she said, making a great show of smacking her lips. "It doesn't taste bad at all."

"You're bad. . . ."

She reached between them for his rigid cock and soon they were locked together, driving at each other until the bed—and maybe the entire hotel floor—shook.

It was late evening of the next day and Jason Sharp was gone. The following morning, Clint and Sandy would be gone, too, in their own separate directions. And Lost City was in the process of being cleaned out.

"The Secret Service sure got someone out here fast," she commented.

"There just so happened to be a Federal Marshal in the area," Clint said. "Or at least that's what I was told."

"There are coincidences in life, you know."

Remembering the two most recent in his life he said, "Don't remind me."

They were in their hotel room, in bed, where they had spent a good portion of their time since arriving in town. There was nothing better they could think of to do, and who knew where they would see each other again.

"What are you going to do with that telegram from the head of the Secret Service congratulating you?" she asked.

"I've already bought a good cigar, and I'm going to use it to light it."

"That's something you should save."

"It's something I can't get rid of fast enough. This is it, this is the last one. No more jobs for the Secret Service after this—and I sent Jim West a telegram to that effect."

"What will he do with that one?"

"Knowing him, the same thing I'll do with this one. Burn it."

"Well, I think we've wasted enough time talking," she said. She turned to him and stroked his smooth jawline.

"You know what?"

"What?" he asked.

"I think I miss the beard."

"*What*?"

"It added something," she said. "It tickled my thighs, and it gave you some character, and it added something to the sex. I think there should be at least one beard in every bed, don't you?"

"Then we've got nothing to worry about."

"Why?"

He reached down and ran his fingers through the hair between her legs, and then made a fist, causing her to start.

"We've still got yours. . . ."

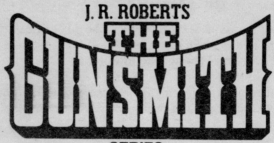

J. R. ROBERTS
THE GUNSMITH
SERIES

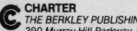